ALONDRA

A.L. HAWKE

PHANTOM HEART, LLC

ISBN: 978-1-953919-18-2 (paperback)

ISBN: 978-1-953919-16-8 (ebook)

ISBN: 978-1-953919-37-3 (hardcover)

Library of Congress Control Number: 2022937294

This is a work of fiction. It comes directly from the author's imagination. Fictional witchcraft is included to infuse a sense of realism to the novel, but in no way is it supposed to represent actual practicing witchcraft, witches or the religion of Wicca. The book also includes fictitious names, characters, places, and incidents. Any public names are used solely for creative purposes. Any resemblance to actual people, living or dead, or to companies, institutions, or locales is entirely coincidental or accidental.

Line edited by Stephanie Marshall Ward

Proofread by Alexa B., alexabooks.wixsite.com/authors

Cover © 2022 by Regina Wamba of MaeIDesign.com

Published by Phantom Heart, LLC

27702 Crown Valley Pkwy D-4, #201

Ladera Ranch, CA 92694, USA

Printed and bound in the United States of America

First printing May, 2022

Learn more about A.L. Hawke at www.alhawke.com

Correspondence: contact@alhawke.com

1

VENITE FORAS

I'm leaving Hawthorne. I keep going over it again and again in my head as I ascend this dark path. My tennis shoes crunch leaves and slosh in the mud. My footsteps are the only sound, except for water pelting the leaves. There's a canopy sheltering me from the downpour. A little. The clouds are stormy, but an occasional sliver of white moonlight slips through the branches above as I walk. To my right, I pass a steep precipice overlooking campus. Far below a few splashes of yellow shine through the woods, lights from our main library at Hawthorne University.

I'm not wearing a coat, and I don't have an umbrella. I'm cold, but I don't care. It's a foregone conclusion that I don't belong here. I'm a friendless freshman surrounded by students burying their heads in books, wearing Greek letters, or sporting thick black makeup.

I mean there's Alondra. She's this goth. She's this girl with long black hair, a sweet smile, and these gorgeous, mesmerizing green eyes...damn. She's hot as hell. I had a crush, but never asked her out. Now that I'm leaving, I suppose I never will.

I enter a break in the trees. But then my trail turns into an even denser path. It grows too dark. I take out my hand-held flashlight. It's a little weird that I'm hiking a trail in the middle of the night. I could slip off the slippery ledge at any moment and die, or be attacked by a black bear or rattlesnake. But I've got this overall screwed-up feeling tonight, you know?

I was never assigned a roommate. That was weird. Some people might love that. Not me, but my absentee roommate sort of puts the whole shitty experience into perspective. I tell you, people are way too cliquey here at Hawthorne. This school is deep in the woods, and if you don't join a group, all the shadowy trees start to feel gloomy as hell.

My grades are fine, I suppose. Maybe I shouldn't complain so much? Perhaps I should just keep to myself and study alone like the rest of the nerds on campus.

Why the fuck am I talking to myself, anyway?

Because it's getting that bad, Lee.

As I traipse up a steeper incline toward the crest of the hill, I freeze—not just from cold. There's rustling in the leaves, but the foliage is too thick to see anything. I guess it's a large animal. But then I hear laughter. I catch a glimpse, through branches, of two people running. The odd thing is they're running through the bushes, not on any of the trails to the hilltop.

They make it through a clearing. They're clearly visible now. I jump back at the sight of their naked breasts and asses shimmering under white moonlight. Their skin is coated in filth. One turns and gazes at me. I can swear there's something smeared over her face. Actually, it covers both of their faces. Their eyes are moving about wildly. They're high off something. The scene is so weird that I look back into the darkness of the woods thinking I must be seeing things.

But then they laugh again.

"*Venite foras!*" cries one. "*Venite foras.*" Then the other echoes, more high-pitched, almost sounding like a bird, "*Venite foras. Venite foras.*"

The two girls run—knee deep in bushes and reeds—up the rest of the slope until they disappear over a ledge, still laughing.

Toward the peak of the cliff, a place called Hilltop Bluff, I smell smoke. And there's a red hue at the summit. I hear more voices. I reach the summit; then I hide behind a bush in a dense thicket. I'm hiding because ten to fifteen girls wearing these weird hooded black cloaks are circling around a huge bonfire. And in the center is another girl, pale, naked, but her body is clean. She is tied to two large wooden beams shaped in an *x*.

"*Lux tenebris!*" cries one of the black-cloaked girls. She is standing at the center of the group, close to the bonfire. They all repeat it. Then one rushes forward holding a large golden chalice out to the girl, "*Lucifer! Lucifer! Satanas!*" She splashes fluid from the chalice onto the girl tied to the stakes.

The tied girl opens her eyes wide and screams in apparent ecstasy, shaking and twitching, now covered in a sticky brownish-red fluid. The girl at the center of the group moves to a table upon which an animal with antlers is trying to squirm out of ropes. As her cloak shifts, I see her naked breasts. All the cloaked girls are nude underneath their cloaks, I think. Then she pulls out a long, curved dagger and strikes the poor animal dead. All of them cry out as if they feel the animal's pain. Then she bends over the animal and smears it with the fresh blood. Is this the fluid I saw on the wild girls?

Another one leaves the circle. The black robe is dropped revealing a naked body, but it's a man's. He has short hair, and his skin is pale. He approaches the girl on the wooden beams. She cries out something inhuman. But she's not crying out in pain or fear. She's gesturing with wild eyes and a free hand for him to approach closer.

"Touch me," she says. "Fuck me. Please fuck me. *Venite foras. Venite. Venite.*"

I look around the hillside, then back to the path I came from, ready to bolt. I can't believe what's happening.

I carefully get up to head back down the dirt trail, but then I hear a scream. I look back at the bonfire. I wish I hadn't. The man is embracing the woman on the planks and flexing his ass tightly, fucking her on this *x*. The sex drives the rest of the people to move quickly in a circle around them, dancing, and bobbing up and down and chanting. The girl on the *x* doesn't seem in pain. She's screaming in ecstasy, goading him further.

I've had enough. I rush back down the trail.

A large animal jumps me... no, it's not an animal. It's one of the girls I saw running through the bushes. She grabs me and trips me, and I fall to the ground on some ivy. I drop my flashlight. Then the other girl appears from behind a bush. Their eyes are roaming wildly over me, lit by white moonlight. I see up close that the liquid covering their faces, including their lips, is not just brown, but red. Blood. It's blood. And it must be fresh to have stuck to them despite the downpour earlier. The blond also has blood staining her hair in auburn streaks. Animal or human?

"Let me go!"

"*Venite foras,*" she says, nodding and gazing at my body with crazed eyes. She's a dark-skinned girl, running her finger along my hair and cheek. A pale girl with long blond hair is on her knees beside her. The blonde is oddly jerky, reminding me of a bird. "*Venite. Delactatio. Venite. Foras. Fructus.*" Then the dark-skinned girl runs her hands under my jacket and along my shirt and all over my stomach, chest, and abs and whispers, *"Fructus. Coitus fructus."* The pale-skinned girl echoes her words quietly with a grin.

The dark-skinned girl straddles me. Her eyes are still wandering everywhere as she's probing me with her fingers as if I were a specimen. Her gaping grin doesn't seem sane. And her hands and limbs are jerking in odd directions over me.

"Like to watch?" asks the blonde nodding beside us. She giggles and grabs one of my arms. I'm trying to slide out of their grasps, but they're pinning me down. It begins to drizzle again.

The one on top of me brings her mud-caked face closer to me and smiles. "You like to watch fucking, hmm?" she asks. "Maybe you want to fuck us?"

My jacket's off; then comes my shirt. The shirt's torn, I think—everything is happening so fast. I jerk desperately, trying to get her off, but they're strong—inhumanly strong. And now the girl over me is grinding into me as if she's having sex with me. Her friend is laughing.

Rain drips down the nude girl sitting on me, but she doesn't seem to notice or care. There's a crack of thunder. Then lightning illuminates her.

Before I can strike her to get her off, both girls haul me up and pull me toward the yellow-red firelight.

"Come fuck us by the fire," says the blonde with a nod, pulling at me and laughing. "Come. *Venite. Venite.*"

The group circling the fire is dancing with their heads bucking up and down, moving around the flames and the central wooden *x* where the couple is fucking. This act, in front of other people, deep in the middle of the woods, before a huge bonfire with circling witches—witches, yes, witches; that's what their laughter is like now...yes, exactly like cackling witches—while I'm being dragged by two beastly girls...

I start pulling the girls with all my might. I lift weights, I'm not weak, but these girls seem inhumanly strong. I lift one of them and throw her toward a tree. But as soon as she falls to the ground, she acts like a caged wild animal and leaps back at me.

I'm in the open grassy field at the top of the summit. I look down and there's blood on my flank. It's not their blood; it's a gash on my stomach from something. A twig that stabbed me? I don't know. Then the pale girl sees it, runs up, touches it, and licks her finger.

"Get away from me, girls. Stop it!"

The goths stop moving in a circle hearing my struggle. Then they all freeze quickly, unnaturally quickly, turn, and stare at me. They're bizarrely perfectly still. The only movement that continues is the man screwing the girl on the planks. And light rainfall. I'm so disturbed by the whole group of black-clothed witches staring at me that I stop resisting. The naked girls beside me see the group too, and they also freeze. Then each of them hooks an arm in one of mine and walks me, still shirtless, to the bonfire.

The couple's moaning is all that's heard in the woods now. Everyone else is as quiet as the rainfall on the leaves of the trees.

"*Venite foras*," the girls in cloaks whisper—just like the two girls who attacked me. "*Venite foras*."

"*Profer extraneo deinceps*," another witch says, raising her hands to the moon with her back turned to me. She has long black hair; she is the only one that hasn't turned and looked at me yet. She's facing the couple fornicating by the fire.

The girl cries out in rapture as the couple climaxes. Then, even weirder, a male witch turns the wooden planks like a wheel so that the girl is hanging upside down before the flames. He leaves her like this, her body still twitching in the firelight, and approaches the witches, grabbing a cloak on the ground. He puts it on and acts like nothing happened.

The dark-haired girl with her back turned to me holds her arms up high before the symbol, as if worshipping the *x* and bonfire. Then she drops her arms and turns. I can see her pale skin, including her boobs, in an opening in her black cloak. She has bright green eyes.

When I recognize the eyes, I cringe. This is my crush. This is the girl I liked in my study class. Then I feel the heavy weight of the crush falling away. It's Alondra. This is Alondra. And when Alondra recognizes me, her familiar emerald eyes open very wide.

"Liam?" she asks, shaking her head violently. "No."

She runs toward me, shouting at me, *"Somnus! Somnus."* She throws her arm before me as if slicing the air. *"Somnus. Somnus."*

I close my eyes. I feel as if I'm falling. I finally stop resisting the two girls holding me and feel them lay me down on the grass.

I wake up with my head in my arms at a study carrel beside a window of the Jonathan Brewster Taylor Library. I'm wearing someone else's long white T-shirt. There's a pain at my right side, and as I touch my skin under the shirt, I feel bandaging. I don't feel hung over. If anything, I feel good. Refreshed.

Outside the window of the brick library, the sky is pink through the thick branches of trees. The sun is either rising or setting. There's no one around me in the library, I'm guessing it's early morning. I check my watch. It's around 8:00 a.m.

2

———

THE PSYCHO KILLER

"Can any of you explain how one controls people? How do you get into someone's mind?"

Professor Kriegel's lecturing. He's a short, bald, overweight eccentric man wearing gray sweatpants and a T-shirt. Right now, he's pacing on the stage under a projected image of Charles Manson, who's sticking his tongue out at us under the tattooed swastika on his forehead. Kriegel's the main reason I chose this elective. Not because of him, but because of his slides. His slides, I tell you, are legendary.

"We talked of Bundy. He murdered for sex, engaging in necrophilia. But he did it looking professional." The slide changes to show Ted Bundy wearing a suit. That's more boring. "He's a similar serial killer to Jeffrey Dahmer, only Dahmer ate his victims." The next slide shows meat and sinew strewn over a table at a crime scene. There are groans from the crowd. This is what I'm talking about. Don't you love it?

He paces under the slaughterhouse.

"Charles Manson manipulated people, but his perversions involved making others do his work. His cult murdered, not him. That was the difference. He was able to get into people's minds and control them."

My professor stands right in front of me, on stage, looking out at the crowd. The lecture hall is packed, and I'm in the front row. The slide changes to a more pleasant picture: a hippie commune. People are sitting around a guy with long hair playing an acoustic guitar on the grass.

I'm having difficulty focusing. I don't know what the hell happened last night. For all I know, I could have been drugged and raped. I was trudging through the doldrums of my loneliness, in my first semester at Hawthorne, thinking of Alondra. Seeing my "crush" was helping me get through my days here. Not anymore. Not after seeing her naked leading a psycho-goth cult.

A picture of a woman unconscious with a plastic bag over her head flashes above. Okay, that's a bit too much. My classmates think so too. Many students groan. He flashes the slide quickly, as if it was never there, to another crime scene.

"But I posit all of our serial killers murdered for control."

Like Alondra? Maybe that's what her hypnotic eyes are all about? Maybe she's a psychopathic killer, like all these serial killers? Maybe the blood last night wasn't animal blood after all?

On cue, a girl wearing a black-checkered skirt with black leggings hurries down the dimly lit aisle. Her red sweater says "Hawthorne," and she's wearing sunglasses. At first, I take little notice, but then she tips down her shades, revealing bright green eyes. She's not in her usual black makeup, but it's Alondra for sure. She smiles and nods at me. I turn away. In my periphery, I catch her quietly sitting down in the only open spot, on the other side of the guy to my right. She puts a stack of books on her desk and takes out a notepad and pen. From the corner of my eye, I watch her carefully preparing for class. I love that. I love watching her obsessively arrange her desk with all her stuff. I don't know why. Maybe it's just because it's her.

The image on the screen changes to another grotesque scene: a bloody body on a white tile floor.

The student to my right, irritatingly, hands me a note.

We need to talk.

In my periphery, I see Alondra leaning forward, nodding, and looking at me. I crumple the note and lean my chin on my hand, completely ignoring her.

"Being a sociopath," the professor continues, "it didn't take much for Manson to learn how to use his grandiosity to impress others. He moved his family from San Francisco to Los Angeles, creating a cult of prostitution and drugs."

Liam, I'm sorry, reads a second note. *You need to let me explain.*

I crumple the second note.

"Manson was a white supremacist preaching that Armageddon was nigh and that a leader, himself, was needed to prevail against the Black Americans before they took over the world. It was with this cult that he used satanic symbols. And much of the satanic panic in the eighties grew out of the acts committed by his commune on August eighth, 1969."

The guy to my right practically throws a CD on my desk. He's pissed about having to pass yet another thing from her. The CD has a cover portraying two girls, one with white wings. It's the new album cover of a grunge band we like. She knows this means something to me. I asked her if I could borrow it during our study group last week. Attached to the plastic case is a yellow sticky note: *You can keep it.*

For a moment I relish looking at her handwriting. If she weren't staring at me, I could do something really stupid like sniff it to smell her perfume.

You love-sick idiot. You're so dumb, Liam.

Well, when I'm hooked, I'm hooked. Even when the girl happens to enjoy standing naked in a druid's cloak, in the middle of the night, raising her hands before a satanic pentagram.

The guy to my right's had enough. He stands up in the aisle gesturing for me to take a seat closer to Alondra. I hesitate but nod and switch seats, because the whole class is literally watching him standing behind me.

Alondra smiles as I sit beside her. She touches my arm and nods. And, fuck me, I can't help but enjoy the smell of her lavender- and vanilla-scented perfume.

"Manson instilled fear of the apocalypse," continues the professor. Alondra is scribbling another note. It's not about the lecture, I'm sure. I roll my eyes. "His victims were runaway teens, porn stars, prostitutes—people who would have looked up to him and followed his psychopathology. Folks, Manson is great for our study of sociopaths." Dr. Kriegel stops right in front of me again. "He used his megalomania not to lure victims, but to control his cult to do it for him. But isn't that the same as Bundy or Gacy?"

This note is kinda long. It reads:

Apologizing for last night is trite. I need to talk to you. Can you meet tonight at my place? If for some reason you can't, call me. I left my phone number on the back. But I think we need to talk about this in person. We'll be alone.

Then she hands me another note:

My friend Jane will be the only other one at the house. She'll let you in.

Liam, I'll tell you everything. I promise. If it helps, I'm sorry.

After I finish reading, she flashes me that irresistible sweet smile that she loves wearing. She tears off another piece of paper and quickly writes and passes it over. *CD's yours.* Then she nods with her same big grin. For a moment, I tell you, I'm lost in those damn mesmerizing green eyes.

"Thanks, but no thanks," I say, putting the CD back on her desk. Alondra furrows her brow but then opens her green jewels wide, turning and gazing up at the stage. Dr. Kriegel is glaring down at us.

"Since you're so chatty," my professor says, with his voice sounding through the speakers throughout the auditorium, "Ms. Billington, what do you think about my theory?"

Who the hell's Ms. Billington? I know the Billington Frat House. That's the most popular building in Hawthorne. They throw a huge Halloween party every year.

"Happy to see you in the front row for once," the professor adds, before she can respond. "Do you think Manson's sociopathic charm was the same sociopathic megalomania of all the other serial killers?"

Neither of us says anything. I think I hear Alondra swallow hard. No, that's me.

"He shot Bernard Crowe in the stomach, professor," answers Alondra, shaking her head. She speaks loudly enough so the whole auditorium can hear her. "Who's to say that Manson was any different? Maybe he would have preferred killing if his hippie commune wasn't at his disposal? Yeah, I agree with you. I think he's the same as all the others."

There's no hesitation in her voice. It's like she's been transformed. And she seems so confident, even though everyone in the auditorium is staring at her.

Then my mouth feels dry when he glances down at me.
Please, Jesus, please don't have him ask me.

"What do you think?"

"I... Uh—"

"That's what he and I were just talking about," Alondra interjects. "We were agreeing with you. He would have been a killer whether he got others to do it or not."

There's silence and Dr. Kriegel lifts an eyebrow.

"What of his own assertion, in interviews, that he did nothing different from our government in Vietnam?" Dr. Kriegel asks. "Isn't war killing?"

"Lyndon Johnson didn't go to war with Vietnam in order to control the American population," Alondra retorts. "He went to war to protect it. Or to protect US power and hegemony."

"But I'm asserting that," Dr. Kriegel continues, "as Manson excused his own actions, perhaps, psychologically, the charisma of a leader is the same as that of a psychopath. Such power might be used for satanism or for good."

"No, I don't think that's the same," Alondra says, shaking her head.

He looks at me and I stupidly just shake my head too. Because I'm not about to dare say a damn thing.

"But I find it offensive and ignorant to assume satanism is simply bad," continues Alondra. I stare at her. "Satanism is primarily anti-Christian. And, anyway, drawing the word "PIG" in blood on a refrigerator is not representative of satanism. That's Hollywood showmanship."

"Isn't satanism evil by the Judeo-Christian definition?"

"If you believe those religions. But that's just not the issue, Professor." Alondra laughs. She brushes her long black hair back from her face. "Really, whether he is anti-Christian is not relevant. What he did is what's important. He confused everyone by pushing a satanic panic. Just as he's confusing you now by excusing his acts of murder by saying they're no different from governing a nation at war."

To this, the whole auditorium gets really loud with scoffs and laughter. Then they break out in applause.

"I wasn't saying it," the professor says with a smirk. "I was asking you."

"Then my answer's no. But he wasn't satanic. He did not properly study rites or perform sabbaths. He used symbols to spread fear over his imagined race war. Honestly, I'm more disturbed by the swastika on his forehead."

There's more applause. I'm wondering if Alondra intends to go on. She's squinting up at Dr. Kriegel, with those green eyes intensely challenging him.

He pauses, continuing to stare down at her. It's tense and the entire auditorium is quiet. "Come up to the front row more often, Ms. Billington," he says finally. Then he's back to pacing.

I take a deep breath.

As confident as my new friend acted, she becomes quiet after her performance. Then she flutters her eyelids and breathes hard. She can't fool me. She was scared.

She turns to me and gives me her classic sweet smile. But her quick change in countenance, this sudden sweet grin—even though, I admit, it turns me on—seems evil. And then I'm thinking, she might claim Charlie Manson isn't satanic, but that doesn't mean she isn't.

At the end of class, we gather our books and I rush out of the lecture hall. She tugs at my arm and I ignore her, moving up the aisle.

Outside, it's gloomy and drizzling. I don't have an umbrella, so I hope it doesn't rain hard.

Alondra is on my tail as I walk under an aluminum awning.

"Nice job showing him his place, Allie," says a short blond girl passing by her. "Are we going to meet tonight?"

I cock my head and see Alondra gesturing at me. "I'll tell you later, Jane."

Alondra pulls my arm again and I finally stop. Then she furrows her brow and searches deeply into my eyes. She's chewing gum. Spearmint—by the smell. She even digs into a pocket and offers me some. I'm glaring at her.

"What time is it?" she asks, breaking her gaze and redistributing her books to her other arm. She glances at the watch on her wrist. It's silver and looks expensive.

"What do you want?" I ask.

She frowns. "Lee, you weren't supposed to be there."

"Is that supposed to make me feel better?"

"No. I'd love to explain to you what happened. That's what I wrote in class."

"You were worshipping the devil?"

"I can't talk about it here." She looks around.

I resume walking. Neither of us says we're gonna walk together, but we do. And neither of us knows where we're going—at least, I don't—so we just sort of meander under the metal awning with other students.

"You don't have that album?" she asks. "Have you heard all of it yet? It's awesome."

"I've heard most of the songs on the radio. Was I drugged last night?"

"No. But I don't want to talk about it here."

I stop by a tree, away from the crowd, and turn from her. Maybe I'm trying to avoid her eyes? "How does Dr. Kriegel know you so well?" I ask. "And why does he call you Ms. Billington?"

"Cause my last name is Billington, silly. And aside from

my family owning this whole boring town, believe it or not, Liam, outside of extracurricular activities, I'm a bit into my books like you. And, apparently, I've visited during his office hours too much."

"Who says I'm into books?"

She just lifts her brow.

Before I can ask any more, she digs through the pile of stuff in her arm and brings out the CD. She pushes it against my chest.

"For god sakes, enjoy it. It's fucking great."

We're no longer under an awning, and the drizzle is turning to light rain. But neither of us goes back under shelter. And I hate to tell you this but, even though I don't want to be, I'm really into this girl. Maybe it's because she's so weird? Or maybe it's because she's so pretty. I really don't know. She's probably just really hot.

I think she's into me.

"Here, Lee. Take it." She pushes the CD against my chest again. "It's cool that we're into the same music. Just take it. And meet with me tonight. I'll explain to you about what was going on at the cliff. I owe you. We'll eat dinner at my place."

I had a girlfriend in high school. Her name was Sandra. Sandra was a straight-A student, pretty but nerdy. It was platonic. This girl's not nerdy, she seems wild.

Is she actually asking me out on a date?

No, stupid, she's trying to cover up her sex cult.

Maybe she's planning on killing me, like Charlie Manson? Or perhaps brainwash one of her goth friends to do it? God, she's got the eyes for it.

Speaking of that, why isn't she wearing her black makeup? Why is she wearing a preppy "Hawthorne" sweater, looking almost like a sorority girl? It's the first time I've seen her look "normal" on campus.

"Lee, I didn't attack you, if you remember."

Oh, that's supposed to make me feel better.

"All right," she says, shaking her head. "Look, it's up to you. I'm inviting you to give me a chance to explain. But I can't talk about it here. I've got to go."

"Was I roofied?"

"I told you, you weren't drugged," she snaps.

"Then how did I get knocked out? Did those girls... have sex with me?"

"No, ah-ight? Look, come to my house. Or..." She turns from me, looking impatient. "Please, Liam. Just come over tonight to my place and let me explain." She looks down. Not just down at the ground—down, like depressed.

"All right."

She glances up and flashes that winning smile. But it looks a little wicked. To be honest, I like it. I told you. I'm hooked.

You're a moron, Liam.

3

SHE'S A WITCH

IT'S POURING RAIN. I PARK MY RED CAMARO IN FRONT OF THE house, behind this nineteenth-century carriage coincidentally matching the color of my car. The carriage is the only other vehicle in the driveway. I thought of turning off the main road, riding down the one-lane road to 75, and driving back home to Raleigh, leaving this freak town forever. But I didn't. Instead, I drove a few minutes from my dorm to this mansion on the hill. Curiosity got the best of me again, I suppose. I want to hear her explanation for what happened on the cliff.

Alondra lives in a grand white house on a hill with a majestic columned porch. I've been here before. She likes to throw parties for the school. God knows what her parents think about that. Unlike the surrounding thick woods, the trees near the house are nicely trimmed and lamps shine over the perfectly mowed lawn. There's even a garden near the porch. Like Alondra, the house is gorgeous.

I take out an umbrella and walk up to the door and knock. The girl who opens is wearing a long saffron dress and no goth makeup. Under the crystal chandelier, she looks like a pretty Southern belle. She's a little older than Alondra. I've seen her. She's the short-haired blonde who talked to Alondra after the lecture. She's always hanging with Alondra. They're like best friends.

"Hi," she says with a kind smile, reaching out for a handshake. "I'm Jane."

"Liam," I say taking her hand.

"Come in." She takes the umbrella and leans it by the door. Then she reaches for my coat. "Allie had dinner made for you. Are you hungry?"

"Are you her butler?" It's a stupid joke, but she laughs. I can smell dinner. It's something like roasted turkey or chicken. It's pleasant.

"She's in the dining room."

"Why can't she answer the door herself?" I ask.

Because she's fucking weird.

"Go to the dining room and you'll see."

What?

I nod as politely as I can and walk down the hall. I look back and Jane's still smiling that nice welcoming grin, gesturing to the left. I turn at the end of the hall and enter one of the most elegant rooms I've ever seen. No lights are on. Just a ton of candles on a dining room table. The room connects to another room—the kitchen, I think—but that room has all the lights out.

Sitting at the end of a long wooden table is Alondra. But she's not dressed like she was in the lecture this morning. She's wearing a black hood over her head with her black druid cloak. As she pulls back her hood, her dark goth makeup is thicker than ever, with black lipstick and black eye shadow. She even drew a black star on her forehead. It kind of reminds me of ash on the foreheads of Christians for Lent. Or the swastika on Charlie Manson's head. (That thought creeps me out.) I have no idea what this star means.

She gestures for me to sit, and I'm about ready to throw one of the candles at her and run back to my car.

"Sit down, Lee. Did you eat?"

"Call me Liam. Lee is a nickname for my friends."

She frowns and flutters her eyelids over that, just like she did after speaking in the lecture hall.

I look down at a magnificent cornucopia on the table—a feast, really. There's a whole chicken, poshly decorated in thin green leaf garnishes, two silver trays of potatoes—one mashed and another roasted—and a plate of carrots and spinach. A fancy crystal decanter is beside it, full of red wine. I point to the wine. "Blood?"

She laughs and shakes her head.

"Are you trying to shock me?" I ask.

"No. I'm trying to explain."

"And having Jane open the door was…?"

"To lighten the impact."

"You think of everything."

She just nods. Then she looks at the window pensively. I follow her gaze.

The window is the most amazing part of the room. It's a wall of glass looking out into the forest. During the day, this room must be spectacular with such a view of the woods. Tonight, it's too dark, but I can still make out the shadow of dense trees. Water drips along the glass, and I can hear the raindrops outside.

"Nice house you have, Allie," I remark. I put my hands in the pockets of my jeans. But I don't sit.

"I was born rich, Liam. And my name's Alondra. The only one who calls me Allie is my best friend."

"Is she a witch too?"

"Of course," Alondra says with a nod. "So you get that I'm a witch?"

"Are you fucking kidding me?"

She permits a chuckle. "Come have dinner with me. I haven't eaten. And I promise you I won't bite."

"Oh, you're not a vampire too?"

She shakes her head. But I don't sit down.

"Did you ever see *The Wizard of Oz*?" I think she thinks that's funny. I don't. It creeps me out with her dark makeup and green eyes.

"Who hasn't?"

"Think of me as Glinda."

"Uh, no. No, no. You're not Glinda. Not after what I saw last night. And honestly right now, you don't look like Glinda either. Sorry."

"Okay. That's fair. But I haven't eaten and I'd enjoy your company. I promise to be nice tonight."

"You're probably more like the witch from Hansel and Gretel."

"I said I won't bite."

My body, more than my mind, walks over to the end of the dining room and slowly sits beside her. I stare out the window facing me. Then I put a napkin on my lap. She smiles at that. God, I love her smile. Why was this witch graced with such an angelic smile? Maybe that makes her more evil?

She gets up, takes a gorgeous piece of chinaware, apparently meant to be my dish, and carves some meat. I enjoy watching her brush her sleeve by me slowly cutting the meat. Not only because she's cutting meat, but also because she seems to be aware of me watching her do it—*me* watching her. Then she spoons some carrots and spinach onto the plate and plops a roll on the side. It'd be elegant, even sexy, her preparing me a dish, if she weren't in a long black witch robe.

She hands me the plate.

"Bon appetite," she says with a smile. Then she picks up

her own plate.

"Should we say grace?"

"You're funny, Lee," she says with a laugh. "You really are a very funny guy."

"It's Liam. Everyone seems to think all you goths are devil worshippers. I thought that was stupid until last night. I've heard bad things said about you and your friends at church. Now I believe them."

"People are ignorant," she says with a shrug. "I hoped to break those misconceptions with you. I hoped that you could realize we're just people."

I shake my head.

She starts to work her food with a fork and knife—real expensive silverware, of course—and I love watching her beside me, cut her potatoes, bring some up to her black lips, and eat. That's how hooked I am. I'm completely enraptured over watching her eat and with her getup, and that scares me. But maybe that fear is alluring too?

She furrows her brow as if reading my mind.

"Did you already have dinner? You're not eating."

"I can't eat with you wearing that cloak."

She nods and obliges me by taking it off and laying it on a wooden chest behind her. Underneath the cloak are an elegant dark blouse and slacks.

I grab a roll and bite into it. It's warm French bread. Very good. I wonder where she got all this great food. Was it shipped from Atlanta? We don't have the greatest food in Hawthorne.

She smiles and demurely pats her lips with a white napkin. Her lipstick stains the napkin black. That's when I notice, oddly, as she twirls her fork in some spinach, that she didn't serve herself any meat.

"So, what would you like to know?" she asks.

"Where should I start? How about why I chose such a

freak college? That's what I kept asking myself when I was out late last night."

"Well, that should be my question to you," she says, after swallowing some spinach. "Well, Hawthorne's a good liberal arts school. You said you were a psych major, right? We have some renowned professors. Dr. Kriegel. He's a history teacher, but there are lots of psych students in our class. And we love his lectures, right? Psychology is a good department. And that's a good crossover class."

"Hawthorne has a good history department."

"Yeah." She raises her brow and nods. "It does. A very good history department. I hope to teach here someday."

I cut into the chicken. It's absolutely amazing, of course. There's a tart sauce, almost orange, on it. It's like the food you get in a really fancy restaurant.

"Did you make this?"

"Hell no," she says with another laugh. "Are you joking, Lee? Sorry...Liam."

"You can call me Lee."

"I can't do much better than PB and J. Or an occasional cheese sandwich. I've tried. Ask Jane when you get a chance. We've burned lots of stuff together, especially when we were little. She's from Hawthorne too, you know. We both grew up here."

"Did that help with you getting in?"

"Possibly." She shrugs. "But I got pretty damn good grades in Flintwood High too."

"Dr. Kriegel thought you were pretty smart."

"Yeah. Look, Lee." She pours some wine from the decanter into my glass but then stops. "Oh, do you drink wine? You're a freshman. You're probably underage?"

"I've had plenty of wine."

"Well, Dr. Kriegel," she says, filling my glass and sitting back down, "he's the best history teacher in school. I'm hoping to work on a dissertation with him, if I can get into the grad program. My dream would be to teach history at Hawthorne."

"Judging by your speech in class, you'd make a great professor."

"You think so? How 'bout you? What do you want to do?"

"I'm considering premed. If not that, I'd love to be a counselor."

"Well, if it's med school, you should transfer. Hawthorne's a great liberal arts college, but stinks for science."

I shrug.

She peers at my face, no, scrutinizes me. I can swear she can read minds with those green gems of hers. I feel my heart quicken as she stares at me.

"Why don't you become a counselor?" she asks, finally breaking eye contact. "You seem thoughtful."

"I don't know." I sip some wine. It tastes sharp. It might be good, but I wouldn't know. I lied to her. I really don't drink wine. "I don't know what I want to do. I almost went in undeclared."

"But you got into the most popular class in school. How'd you manage that as a freshman?"

"I have a scholarship. I can take any class I want."

"Smart." She nods. "I knew you were smart."

I pick up my fork again, but then I decide to ask her a more pressing question. "Why do you and your friends wear black makeup?"

She sips some wine pensively. Then she nods and says, "Goth represents death. Black clothes and black makeup represent mourning. I suppose we could wear white shrouds but, by tradition, most cultures wear black to funerals. Unlike our society, we goths don't live lies. We're real. We're not about bullshit. We know our deaths are nigh.

And what many don't understand—including you, perhaps —is that by embracing death, we goths, we witches, live more in one day than many of you in a lifetime. We cherish every waking moment. While all of you outside the occult waste every day pretending like your breath will never cease."

I swallow some meat because that's a mouthful.

She chuckles. "What else would you like to know?" She forks a carrot and smiles at me.

I look around the room. The walls are covered in flickering candlelight. Then I look behind me. The lights are off in the hallway. It's a bit creepy. It reminds me a little of an old horror movie—like I'm expecting a zombie to be lurking behind me in the shadows.

"I think you scare us." *Or you scare me.*

"Because we bring to light the darkness you fear. But you know, Lee, death is an illusion. Your being, who you are, Liam, or Lee, is nothing. You're simply a shell that's taken in thousands of memories. Most of those memories have already faded. You don't mourn for them. If you lose a thousand more, what's to mourn? So what use is fearing death? We are made up of atman: everything that surrounds us. Our individuality and our fear of losing it is an illusion." She sighs and forks some carrots. She squints at her plate, as if pondering it, for a moment. "I think of this stuff a lot."

"What?"

"Death. Do you remember the first day you crawled? Or the first day you rode a bike? Or the first day your mother suckled you? Witches believe in a central soul that passes to the Summerland. But even this is universal. The Hindus call the one soul atman, and I have extended atman to the teachings in my group."

Her group? What sort of a group does she teach?

I stare out the window. The rain has calmed to a drizzle,

but a fog has rolled in, darkening it even more. It's so black. Mysterious. Frightening. It's like her.

"A witch enjoys nature," she says. "A witch enjoys pleasure from nature. And, with it, sacrifice with pain."

I spoon some mashed potatoes.

She looks into my eyes again and, for a moment, I really don't give a shit about her philosophy. I'm entranced, no aroused, by her. And I think she is with me.

Then I'm cursing myself for liking this girl. She's smart? So? She's philosophical? So? She walks around thinking she's a character from a black-and-white Hollywood movie. Deep discourse doesn't get rid of the fact that she's really, really, really weird. And her group of goth weirdos is anything but honest. They are occult. Secretive. Isn't that why I'm here tonight?

"You're always thinking, aren't you, Liam?" she asks. She puts down her fork and knife and leans forward. "What are you thinking about?"

You. But I say, "Nothing."

"We witches," she says, sipping some wine, "walk around being one with atman. Living. And as goths, we live life, not hide from it."

I rub my eyes over that.

"What's wrong?" she asks.

"All you do is hide," I say, shaking my head. "Alondra, I saw you naked in front of a pentagram. On the pentagram was a naked girl tied to two stakes while being screwed. Afterward, she was turned upside down to represent a backward pentagram. I know damn well what that symbol means. That is satanic. Evil. You all act very fake, with your goth makeup, not real at all. Many of you are using it as if it's a costume. And now you're philosophizing about—"

"That's why you're here. To let me explain."

"But what's there to explain? I don't care about your

philosophy. I would much rather know what the hell was going on last night."

"Sit down, Lee."

I didn't even realize I'd gotten up.

"Please."

I take a deep breath and run my hand through my hair.

"What you saw last night was an accident—because you saw it," she says. "You weren't supposed to. I asked you here to... Please, sit down," she says again.

I won't.

"I invited you here to ask you to please not talk about what you saw to anyone."

"I see. That's why I'm here."

"No," she says, shaking her head with a big sigh, "you're also here because I wanted to have dinner with you."

"I don't believe you. Why should I trust you?"

"Why should I trust you? Lee," she says, raising a hand. "What you saw was Capper and Rachel against the stakes. They both agreed to come together in union for our ceremony. They chose to have ceremonial sex. It was completely mutual. Even before mandragora, they agreed to be one under Selene. It was a full moon between the clouds, if you didn't notice."

"I can't do this," I say, shaking my head. My legs are moving me to the door. It's weird, because as much as I'm enthralled by her, my memory of what I saw last night trumps all else and I want to get the fuck out. But, boy, as I'm at the threshold, I hesitate. I...really...do.

Alondra gets up. "If you give me a second. I'm trying to explain."

"Okay."

"But sit down. Please."

"Why?"

I walk over to the window and run my hand over my short hair again.

"You asked why we wear gothic makeup and cloaks, and I told you."

"You lied. You're not real. You all hide behind your makeup."

"I won't hide from you. I can explain what you saw last night."

"No. What I saw disgusts me. I'm not sure I want to know any more. I saw blood on the two girls who attacked me..." I sigh and lean my forehead against the glass, staring out at the mist covering the tree trunks. "At least tell me this, Alondra. And be honest. Did you drug me?"

"You already asked me that. I didn't. I cast a spell on you. I'm a witch. I put you to sleep by using magic."

What...the...fuck?

That's actually much worse.

I turn my head. She's sitting again, with her goth face lit by all the flickering candles along the table. Now she's folding her arms. She's not smiling. She's frowning. She seems as mad as I am. *Did I upset her? Really? Me?* She's telling me she knocked me out with some kind of magic spell. How can I believe that?

"I like your feathery hair," she says, regaining a smile. "It's brown, but almost red."

"Jesus, Alondra, how did you *put a spell on me*?"

"You said we hurt people. By accident, sometimes. But you said we are fake. We're not. I haven't lied to you, Liam. We are real witches. This outfit is not a costume. I cast a spell on you to get you away from those girls. To make you unconscious so that none of the other girls would touch you. We're highly charged when we're in a trance. Mandragora is like an aphrodisiac. Even I can barely control myself under its power. We were drugged, not you. The two girls holding you brought you over to have sex with you. They were drugged—again, by choice. When I saw it was you, I cast a spell on you and made you fall asleep."

"And the satanic pentagram?"

"Good eye." She nods. Then she sips some wine and turns from me. "You're so sharp. We were worshipping the devil. Yes. Sometimes we do that. I'm not Christian. I don't really care about Satan. For me, Satan is just another god, and I really don't care about whether he is good or evil. But some of our members are very religious. That gives that symbol great power. Some of the girls like Satan. Cap does. We also worship natural goddesses, like Hecate. Hecate's not a very nice god either, by the way." She looks back and smirks at my expression. She shrugs. "You want to know why I appeared to you as a witch tonight? It was because this is the real me. Tonight, it's about honesty. I told you. It's trust. You want to know me, here I am. Alondra. I'm a witch. I practice real magic. I've been doing it since I was eight. It's not an act. I'm not just playing with black clothes and makeup. This is not bullshit. This is real magik with a *k*. You might not want to believe it. Then explain everything you've seen. I didn't drug you, but my words put you to sleep. How did I do that? If it was drugs, did you feel a hangover? I'm telling you because I owe you. If I'm honest and tell you the truth, hopefully, I can put your mind at ease."

I lean my forehead on the window again and don't say a thing. It's raining again. The water splashes against the glass.

"But we are occult. Our secrets are secrets. We don't go about telling everyone. I'm honest with you, but with you alone, because I owe it to you, Lee, to explain what happened. I want to explain so that I get your assurance that you won't tell anyone. That's truly why you're here."

Not because she wanted to have dinner with me.

I watch the water run down the windowpanes again. The glass is cold. Winter's coming. Soon it will snow.

I can't believe I'm here. I'm with this odd girl in this amazing rich house. And she wants me to believe she's a witch. More like a schizophrenic. I've got a crush on a hot, rich, psychotic girl.

What happened to me last night? If I don't believe her, she drugged me. And that's repulsive enough to make me want to run. So now I ask myself: *why did you come here, Liam? If this girl drugged you last night at Hilltop Bluff, why did you come and accept her invitation to her home in the first place?*

"I also like you," she adds. "You're cute. Can you come back to the table and sit with me?"

"You're manipulating me," I say, turning back to the window and shaking my head.

"I'm not."

"Can you prove to me you're a witch?"

"Yes. But people don't believe magic even when they see it."

"Try me."

She nods.

"Tenebris," she says, running her hand beside a candle on the table. It is snuffed out.

I smile and shake my head. "You could have blown it out with the flick of your palm. That's a simple parlor trick."

She nods and folds her arms. Then she says plainly, "*lux.*" The candle relights. This time, she didn't move at all.

"It still could be a trick."

"I told you it wouldn't be enough. But if you hang with me long enough, you'll be convinced. I even sometimes attend summonings. I visit haunted houses and help people who have problems with the outer worlds. You can see plenty of magic there, if you want."

"I don't."

She shrugs and picks up her fork and knife and cuts some carrots. Then, with her mouth full, she looks up at me and says, "I think you do. I think you like dark stuff. I think that's why you accepted my invitation to my house."

"What makes you think that?"

She rolls her eyes and points at me with her fork. "You picked a psycho killer class." She swallows some food and shrugs. Then she says, with her mouth full, "You like freaky stuff. I invited you here because we're a secret cult. We're not Wiccan. We practice occult ceremonies, worship the devil, and sometimes engage in ceremonial sex." She sips some wine. "I didn't want to explain your complaints to administration." She forks more potatoes. "But I also..." She looks right at me with her infamous gaze and says, "like you. That is truth. I'd like to be your friend, Lee."

But after that, she decides to stop tending to me. She just tends to her plate and eats, acting like she could spend the rest of the night alone, if that is my wish. I think she believes her trap is set. I'm snared. It is very pompously *her*.

There's a presence about her. Arrogance? Omnipotence? I'm not sure. But she holds so much confidence. More so than anyone I've ever known.

Of course, she's right. I sit back down beside her feeling defeated. She's snared me. Hell, I was trapped even before coming to the house.

But I feel...happy. Happier than ever to be sitting next to her.

"May I?" she asks. She reaches over to touch my hair and I back up. She laughs and tries again. I let her run her fingers along my bangs. "I really like your hair."

"I really like your eyes."

"I hate my eyes," she says, covering them and spooning some mashed potatoes. "They're weird."

"No offense, Alondra, but *you're* weird."

"But I'm right, aren't I? You didn't just choose a serial killer elective because of the professor. You chose it because it deals with what both you and I like thinking about. Death. You're a goth, Liam. Inside, you're a goth. You might not wear black makeup, but inside you're the same as me. I saw it the first time I laid eyes on you, at the welcoming party at my house. Then again in our study group. And I've liked you since. It'll just be my job to add a little actual eyeshadow to your face to bring it out."

"You'll never do that."

"Your loss." She chuckles and shrugs.

I cut some chicken and fork it into my mouth. All the while, she quietly eats her vegetables.

"Where's your parents?" I ask.

"Dead. Mom and Dad died when I was little. A hunting accident, they said, but there was evidence of evil witchcraft. That's one of the reasons I visit hauntings and seek the supernatural. You think I'm bad? There are some really nasty beings out there, Lee. Of course, I don't have proof, but I'm searching. I know my parents were not killed by accident."

I force some tart red liquid down my throat over that one.

"My Uncle Hanley's raised me. He has a farm nearby, in Flintwood, and he's let me live here alone since I graduated high school. He says it's my house, anyway. But trusting me is probably not a great idea knowing what you know about my parties. He doesn't know." She laughs. "He'd disown me if he knew his favorite niece is practicing witchcraft. But he's barely ever here. He doesn't care much for Hawthorne."

"Why?"

"Because it's where my parents died in a *hunting accident*."

"Oh."

"Yeah. Life's a horror show. Wake up, open your eyes, and witness our purgatory. That's what we witches do." She drinks some wine, mulling that over. "How 'bout you, Lee? You're so nice. Where's little Lee's mum and dad?"

"I was adopted. I was raised in Raleigh."

"A horror show," Alondra says, wagging a finger at me. "Life's a fucking horror show. When you see it, one day I will convince you to wear makeup."

"I don't think so."

"Too bad," she says, drinking more wine. "You'd look good."

"So you have this whole house to yourself?"

"Yep."

"Like Pippi Longstocking," I say quietly, more to myself.

"Huh? Yeah, like Pippi," she says. "Only you're the one with the red hair. You think that magical girl with the long red pigtails was happy?" Then she reaches over the table and touches my hand. She shakes her head. "I tell you, we've got a lot in common."

I look into her eyes. She smiles and I feel something in my chest.

"Two orphans," she says, raising her brow. "No family." She raises her wine glass in a toast. "Well, to you and me, Lee."

I raise the glass and drink. I can't hide a wrinkle of my nose.

"You don't drink wine, do you?" she asks with a smirk.

"How'd you know?"

She shrugs. "This is expensive. And very good." Then she touches my hand again. "Can we be friends?"

"Maybe."

"Even after what happened?"

"Maybe. Thank you for dinner, Alondra."

She forks some potatoes to her mouth, nods, and smiles

demurely while looking down at her plate. I finally just eat. But mostly, I enjoy eating quietly beside her.

As I drive back to my dorm, I don't think about the naked girls with blood and grime on their faces who abducted me, or bonfires with satanic symbols. Or witches and all the goths hanging around campus. I think about her. And I consider how this is the best night I've had at Hawthorne. No. I think it's one of the best nights I've ever had.

4

THE POOL

"Did you listen to the song "Quiet" yet?"

"What?" I grab her hand and help her across a stream. The water's pretty deep here, but hikers have tossed a bunch of rocks and logs in the water. It's slippery so we have to be careful. I watch her carefully land her white tennis shoes on the stones. Her legs are so pale. Above her white legs are her cut-off blue jeans and a cute T-shirt, tied above her waist revealing her belly button. She's wearing large dark sunglasses, which is too bad. I can't look into her mesmerizing eyes. I'm wearing blue jeans too, but mine aren't cut into shorts, and I have on a black T-shirt. It's a warmer day with clear skies. I'm shading my eyes from the sun's rays with my Braves hat.

"How much longer?" I ask.

"Not far. So, did you? Did you like that song by Smashing Pumpkins?"

"Yeah. I liked it."

"I knew you would," Alondra says with a smile. "It's funny, right? Billy Corgan's, like, saying to be quiet, but the guitar and drums are blaring in your ears. It's so Smashing

Pumpkins. Did you listen to the whole album? When did you listen to it?"

"I was studying. I have a portable CD player."

"Cool," she says. Then she puts out her hand for me to help her over another stream. "Water's up higher after the rain. Sometimes you can just run across this. You know, I actually like the song "Today" on that album the best. You know what I picture when I hear that song?"

"Hmm?" I ask, pulling her across.

"I see in my mind a music box. The guitar sounds like a music box. So before the guitar and drums blare, I'm picturing a baby looking curiously up at a mobile. It all kinda surrounds this baby. I have a vivid imagination, you know."

"That's for sure."

"Hey!" She hits my shoulder. "What's that supposed to mean?"

"All your friends wear hooded cloaks."

She shrugs.

We walk down a hilly dirt path that only she knew where to find. Then it opens into a meadow of tall yellow grass. We leave the dirt path and cross the meadow. I'm just following Alondra. She's showing me the way. If she left at this point, I'd be totally lost. But I have the feeling that if I blindfolded her, she could feel her way around.

"Alondra, this yellow meadow is kind of like the video," I say. "The video's about an ice cream man in a desert. The grass looks yellow like the desert."

"Really? Never saw the video," she says with a shrug.

"How far are we from your house?"

She stops and puts her finger to her cheek. She turns around, peers across the trees, then shrugs. "You know, I have no fucking idea. I think we're lost."

"We're lost?" I ask, wide-eyed.

She nods with a bigger smile.

"Bullshit. You said you've lived at this house all your life."

She bursts out laughing. "Your brains make my antics less fun," she says. "So the video's in a desert, huh? Go figure. I always pictured a baby in a crib. And you said an ice cream truck? What happens?"

"They repaint the white truck all kinds of colors. And lots of people make out with camera tricks making it look like they're having sex. And the ice cream man looks happy at the end—like, happily ever after not having to sell ice cream ever again."

"I'll have to check this video out. I don't watch a lot of TV. It doesn't sound like what I had in my mind at all."

"No, you're not all that far off. An ice cream truck can play music like a music box."

At the end of the meadow, there are dense trees again. Somehow she finds another dirt path. Of course she does. The woods get thick again and much darker.

"How long have you known this trail?" I ask, stopping and taking a break.

"Since I was a little girl." She looks around at the trees surrounding us. "My dad used to take me."

"Before the accident."

"Uh...yeah." She lifts her eyebrows over her shades.

"Sorry."

"Forget it. My dad loved walking trails with me when I was a little girl. That's why all my memories of him are here. He used to tell me how much he loved Hawthorne. The woods. Mom loved it but didn't like taking me as much. These trails wind so far that if you turn up ahead... See that light in the break in the trees? Over there?" She points. "If you take that trail for another half mile, you'd be right back to campus. And then..." She puts her finger to her black lips. (The lipstick is the only goth makeup she has on this morning.) "If you were to continue further on the trail, you'd land at the Billington Frat House, but we're not going that far. All the trails connect with one another, and my dad told me once that my family owned all the acreage surrounding the Billington House and the college. Not the college itself, but the surrounding woods. My family's been here for hundreds of years." She turns and just looks at me. "How do you like that? You just got to Hawthorne, and you found the heir to the whole goddamn place."

"Can I kiss you?"

"That's random." She shrugs. "But sure. Only if you're good."

I close in pressing my lips against hers. She laughs as my face hits her shades. She takes the sunglasses off. Looking at her mesmerizing eyes, I lose my smile. She turns serious too. Then I lean down again.

I feel her lick my lips and part them. Then I feel her hands run along the back of my head, running through my hair. I hold her tighter. We make out in the woods. It's not the most romantic place. It's dark under the trees. But we're alone and that's nice.

"Come on," she says, putting her shades back on. She tugs at my elbow. "Enough funny business, ah-ight? I want to show you somewhere where it'll be better."

"How was my kiss?"

She shrugs. But then she sticks her hand out for me to hold as we walk on.

I hear the water before I see it. The branches and trunks of this part of the forest are so thick that I can't see much of anything except Alondra and the dirt path between thickets.

"So you've always lived in that house?" I ask.

"Yeah."

"Why does your uncle let you live there alone?"

"It's my house."

"When was your parents' accident?"

"When I was six. And it wasn't an accident. Two people don't get shot in the woods together because someone accidentally thinks they're both deer. I didn't even buy that at six."

"That's terrible."

She nods. "Come on." She tugs at me, leading me down a windy narrow path. "It's just beyond those trees. And…" She gestures at a tunnel of trees, with a big smile, still holding my hands. "Here we are."

I lean down to kiss her lips again. She blocks my lips with her hand and signals with her finger for me to walk with her through the tree tunnel.

I'm speechless. Beyond the tunnel is a large waterfall and a pool surrounded by trees. Rays of light are falling through the leaves and branches of the towering forest. And surrounding the pool are bushes. I feel like I've been transported to a tropical island. It's like a private pool, only it's completely natural.

"So?" she asks. "What do you think?"

"Incredible."

"Yeah," she says, nodding. She removes her backpack. Then she puts her arms around me. "Better here. Ah-ight? Now where were we?" And she puckers stupidly for me.

"Can I be honest with you?" I ask.

"You don't have to ask me every time you do something intimate, Liam." She chuckles. She kisses me again. "Actually, I adore it. It's kinda cute. What?"

"When I was walking the trails around Hilltop Bluff that night, I was seriously considering leaving Hawthorne. There was nothing here for me. Now you show me this. It's like… I can't believe my eyes."

"Pretty cool, huh," she says with a nod, looking back. "Hungry?"

"It's only ten."

"That's what I thought."

She kisses my lips again, entering my mouth. Then she starts stripping in front of me. She removes her shirt and pulls down her shorts. I'm surprised at what's underneath—a yellow bathing suit. She tears herself away from me, pops off her tennis shoes, pulls off her socks, and walks barefoot to the ledge.

"You're kidding?" I ask. "It's probably fifty degrees in there."

She shrugs. Then she walks right up to the water's edge. She dips her toes in the water. "Fifty? How 'bout... forty?"

She leans toward the pool until she falls in.

But as quickly as she falls, she leaps up, splashing and crying, "*Cold!*". She grabs for the ledge. "So fucking cold!"

"Why are you doing this?"

"Fuck! It's cold." She splashes me. The water is freezing. "Come in."

"I don't have a bathing suit."

"You're a boy. You have underwear, right?"

"You can't be serious?"

"Shit." She squints, looking around at the murky water. "I think I lost my shades. I can't find them. I think they're under me. Wait a minute."

She dips her head in and submerges back into the water.

I've already removed my cap and shirt. I'm hesitating with the jeans though. It's warm outside but there's a cold breeze, chilling my bare chest.

Then I worry. She dipped her head underwater and hasn't come up after, like, twenty seconds. Could she be drowning? In freezing water?

Remember Hilltop Bluff, Liam? A month ago, you were telling yourself how bored you were. Now you have a stunning girl asking you to swim with her in a private pool in the middle of nowhere.

So after another ten seconds, I jump in, but with my pants on. The minute I'm in, she jumps up by my side gasping for air. It's shallow and I can stand up beside her. She tosses her shades near her bag, grabs the ledge, and pulls herself onto her elbows. Then she turns to me and bursts out laughing in my face.

"You're crazy."

That's when I feel the cold. It's like someone dropped a bucket of ice over my head. My eyes bulge. *"Fuck, it's cold!"*

She nods and laughs harder. Then she throws her arms around me again, facing me. She's shaking in my arms. She stares at me with those green eyes. And smiles.

"Fuck!" I cry. "It's cold. It's fucking freezing in here!"

"Yeah." She nods. "It's probably fifty."

"How did you hold your breath for so long?"

"I'm a witch." She shrugs. "And I had to get you in." Then she runs her hand along my butt. "Hey, you cheated. You're wearing your pants!"

"It's too cold."

"Do you have any idea how cold you're gonna be on the way back, dummy? Why don't you listen to me?"

"You planned this, didn't you?"

She smiles slyly.

"How did you find this place?"

"It's warmer in the summer." Her teeth chatter. "Then we could actually swim. I've wandered the whole area many times. I told you, this is my home."

"I think we should get out."

She shakes her head. Before I can say another word, she presses her shaky lips onto mine hard. Her tongue enters my mouth and we French kiss. That's nice. And unpleasant. I'm cold. It's like that really loud Smashing Pumpkins song she was talking about: "Quiet." It hurts and is pleasurable at the same time. Kissing her—I think it's the greatest pleasure I've ever experienced in my life. I absolutely love it. And I don't want the pleasure to ever go away. But the frigid water is sharp and cuts at me, hurting me.

"I got sandwiches from the campus store," she says between kisses and our trembling. "And Coke. You...like my pool?"

"I love it."

"I knew you would."

5

____

EMF 101

Dating a witch is not all that different from dating a normal girl. I mean, on one hand, if you're not one yourself, you can't see her on their Sabbath. That means Friday nights are never date nights. And then there was that awkward moment when one of her "sisters," Rachel, the girl that was tied to stakes, ran up to Alondra while we were eating sandwiches on the campus lawn and asked her for the perfect herb to help with her stomach cramps—the answer was gentiana. She's always helping her witches with stuff like that. Other than that, and getting used to her black clothes and eye shadow, she isn't much different from my girlfriends back home. In fact, I think the mystery of Alondra makes her more alluring.

We never have "dates." Just like she doesn't like the word "kiss." But we go out all the time, alone, to nice restaurants and watch movies together. But they are never "dates." Most of the time Alondra calls me at my dorm and we hang at her place. She says she likes hanging with her *friend*. Her friend that she also likes making out with, not "kissing".

That's why I'm excited when she asks me to accompany

her to dinner in a suburb of Macon on Saturday. She won't tell me what it's about, so I guess it could be a "date." I dress the part in a burgundy-striped button-down and slacks and drive her through the woods to the town nearest to Hawthorne. But I was a bit suspicious when she brought her cloak and wore a very witchy black dress with full-on goth makeup.

"Mind telling me where we're going?" I ask.

"A haunted house." She looks over with a wry grin. Then she laughs and touches my arm.

"So... it's a joke?"

"Nu-uh."

Bentmont is a small suburb on the outskirts of Macon. I find it a bit woodsier than the city when a sign directs me to turn into a canopy of trees. That reminds me of school. But soon we enter suburbia, with rows of driveways and two-story homes. It's sprinkling rain and I've been running the windshield wipers on and off over the past hour. It's also foggy and the streetlights are glowing yellow.

"When you said we'd be together tonight, I gotta tell you, Allie, I was expecting a nice restaurant near campus."

"I know," she says with a laugh. "And you look really cute for it."

"Mind telling me why you didn't tell me we were seeing ghosts tonight?"

"Do you know what the word *mundane* means?" She laughs again and touches my arm. "Come on, I warned you about who I am when you visited my house our first night." Then she pecks my cheek and grabs my hand. "You're so cute. There's a couple of real good friends I want you to meet. I've known them since high school. For years now, I've met them all over the state, investigating the paranormal. I was really excited when they told me of some activity so close to home. You keep wanting me to prove my witchcraft. Well, I thought it'd be fun to check this out."

"Fun?"

"You can drop me off if you prefer."

"We're a bit far from Hawthorne."

"I'm a big girl."

I shake my head.

Alondra laughs and touches my arm. "You're such a good sport."

"How often do you go on these haunts?"

"Every month or so. A lot of people ask for help from the Hawthorne witch."

"Why do you seem so chipper about it?"

"Because I love it, Lee."

"I'm not sure if I should be scared or excited."

"Excited," she says, nodding. She stares back at the windshield, holding my hand.

This street in Bentmont looks new. She starts rattling off turns from a map on her lap. Then we reach a very ordinary looking cul-de-sac. She points to a two-story house. "There, Lee."

The only thing spooky about the house is that more fog is rolling in. There's a lot of mist around a single yellow streetlight by the curb. It's beside a large tree in front of the house, a bike leaning against it. A trash can sits by the curb, and a short paved walkway leads through a well-groomed lawn to the front door. A blurry glow emanates from one of the first-floor windows. Otherwise, the house seems covered in darkness. It looks normal enough, sans this really big beat-up gray van parked by the curb.

"They're here," Alondra says, gesturing to the van.

She pulls off her seatbelt, grabs her cloak from the back seat, and jumps out. Then she knocks on the back door of the van. She throws the cloak on and fixes her long dark hair as she waits. Then an overweight guy with a bushy beard opens the two back doors.

"Alondra Billington," he says, jumping out and giving Allie a big hug. Then he turns to me and nods.

"Hey, Alondra," shouts another guy, deeper in the van. "What's up!" The van has a violet hue inside, and I can make out three large TV monitors. The guy closer to the driver's seat is lanky with pale skin, and he's wearing a multicolored Rastafari hat.

"Liam, this is Ray, the leader of this debacle," Alondra says, gesturing to the overweight guy. Then she gestures to the man in the rainbow hat. "And that's David. Guys, this is my good friend, Liam, I was talking to you about."

"Any friend of the head witch of Hawthorne is a friend of mine," Ray says. Then he shakes my hand and winks at me. "Come inside and have a look around. You like computers?"

I shrug. Then I take a gander.

The van reminds me of a hiding place for a police stake-out. There are wires strewn all over the floor, along with fast food bags over stacked metal boxes, and various cameras and camcorders. All three monitors are turned on, lighting up rooms with blotches of yellow, red, and purple. Ray crouches with Alondra over the screens. Then David starts typing on a large keyboard near the front seats.

"Is this the real thing?" Alondra asks him. There's a bed and desk on the screen. It appears to be a bedroom—and everything is in a dark purple hue. She's lost her mirth and has suddenly become very serious.

"That's Maybelle's room. She's thirteen. We think she's the vessel."

"Alice and Maybelle, you said," Alondra says with a nod. Then she moves down to another screen—two figures are sitting on a couch. The figures are blotches of yellow and red. "And there they are?"

"Yep, waiting for the Hawthorne witch," Ray says with a nod. Then he turns to me. "You hang 'round Alondra long enough, man, and you won't question the afterlife anymore."

"Why?" Alondra asks, still staring. "I still do."

She looks back at the bedroom. Then she glides a finger over the final screen. This is just a dark purple hallway.

"Is this infrared?" I ask.

"Good eye, Liam," Alondra says with a nod. "Yes, they're thermal cameras."

"Doesn't that cost a fortune?"

"Yeah," Ray says. "It does. So do the computers. It's good to be in the company of Alondra Billington."

"I sponsor their little ventures, Lee," Alondra says, staring at the bedroom again. "Believe me, if I had a choice I'd be out hunting with these guys—if I wasn't trying to make something of my future."

"Hey!" cries David, looking up from his keyboard. Ray looks at her with a frown. Alondra laughs.

"Is this the real thing or not, Raymond?" Alondra turns back to the monitor.

"I wouldn't waste your time if it wasn't," Ray says with a big smile. "I've seen thermal energy plop itself right down on the desk chair three times over the past twenty-four hours. I've seen small hovering balls of light. Then I've seen light rush across the room. I have the footage, if you care to look."

"No," Alondra says, shaking her head. "I want to see it for myself. Introduce me to the vessel."

Raymond moves to the front of the van and grabs a large camcorder. Then he pats David on the shoulder and gestures for him to move out with him.

They walk with us to the front door of the house, their hands full carrying silver metal boxes and wires. The door's unlocked. David pushes the door open with his foot.

The lighting inside the house has a bit of an orange hue. I see a kitchen and living room to my right, and carpeted stairs to my left. I recognize the living room immediately when I see two women on the couch. They were seen in infrared on the van monitor. One is a teenager, Maybelle, I'm guessing, and the other looks to be in her midthirties. The first thing that strikes me about this "normal" home is that, even though, seemingly, every light is on, it *feels* dark. It not only feels dark; it feels creepy. I feel something in the air. And it seems like there's a dark corner in every room. I don't like it.

The mom and daughter seem very shy. They're wearing glasses. The woman has long curly hair; the girl's hair is short and blond. The woman gets up to greet us, but she backs up, seeing my girlfriend. It's probably Allie's witch cloak and makeup.

"Alice, these are the experts I was talking about," Raymond says. He lays down a large metal box in the foyer.

Alondra nods and smiles. "You have a beautiful home, Alice."

"Thank you. Would you two like some tea?"

"Sure," Alondra says.

"Well, come in, Alondra," says David excitedly to both of us. "Come in."

Alice gets up to get tea from the kitchen, separated from the living room by a half wall room divider. I sit down on an old brown corduroy recliner across from the sofa.

Alice hands me a cup of tea. Then she sits down in the center of the sofa with Alondra on one side and Maybelle on the other.

"You're the Hawthorne witch?" Alice asks.

"In secret," Alondra says with a quick grin. "Yes. You must keep my secret—as secretive as you wish this haunting to be."

Alice and Maybelle nod.

"When did the ghost first appear?" Alondra asks, sipping her tea. It's Earl Gray—a bit soothing in the midst of all the tension.

"Five months ago. Every day. Five months."

"Has the spirit ever hurt you?"

Alice pushes back her blond hair and nods. Holding her hair, she shows Alondra a red mark along her neck. "I get marks like this every morning."

"We took photos," interjects David.

"Did anything happen before your husband's death?" Alondra asks, examining the burn marks. "Were there hauntings back then too?"

"Well...there were sounds at night. This house has always been strange."

"How so?"

"Creaking sounds. Banging. Cracking along the foundations. We never thought much of it. The house was built thirty years ago."

"There's a ton of electric lines going through the nearby field in the backyard, Alondra," David chimes in. He's digging in a duffel bag, sorting through bulbs and batteries, I think. He pulls out a small Polaroid camera. "And there's evidence of water running beneath the surface of the ground."

"Did you check the soil content?" Alondra asks Raymond.

"Loam," says Ray, sitting in a lounge chair at the opposite corner of the room. "Nothing special. No limestone."

"But there's water running below," Alondra says with a nod.

"What does all that have to do with anything?" I ask.

"EMF," Alondra replies. "Electromagnetic fields. EMF fields can be invisible to our senses. Hauntings are either ghosts or demons, Lee. We believe ghosts manifest from an electromagnetic field in a house. Are they illusions or real? I don't know." Then she turns back to Alice. "Your house might not have limestone or chalk, but it's chock full of— excuse my pun—objects that create energy. The running water underground and the nearby power lines could be the cause."

"It's not real?" asks Maybelle.

"Oh, it's very real," Alondra says. "The energy serves as a gateway. There are some hallucinations that are more psychological in nature, but I don't believe a haunting can exist purely from energy. I think it takes both the EMF and the history and setting of the dead to create ghosts—if ghosts are what we're dealing with here. From what I've heard, it sounds like poltergeists." Then she leans over to Maybelle, who spontaneously lurches back. I'm so used to Alondra's weirdness that her getup doesn't faze me anymore. "Poltergeists are ghosts that do violence, like the burn marks on your mom. And you, Maybelle, might be the cause of it."

"What? What do you mean?" snaps Alice.

"Many researchers, including my team, believe that poltergeists can be more a manifestation of psychic energy than ghosts. Teenagers, particularly teenage girls, have a great deal of pent-up energy when maturing. Not only are they learning how to cope in our world, but in the spirit world as well. Psychic energy at this time is extremely powerful. When you add her age to the physics of this house and the stress of the recent loss of your husband, you have a situation ripe for poltergeists."

"We're Christians," Alice says, shaking her head. "We don't believe she can have psychic energy."

"He doesn't believe either," Alondra says, pointing to me. "And he's Christian too. That's why I brought him."

"Oh, you will after tonight, man," says David, slapping my shoulder with a laugh. "You guys ready? Everything's set. We're ready upstairs when you are, Alondra."

Alondra nods.

Alice just puts her head in her hands. Maybelle rubs her back. "It's okay, Momma."

"Tell me some of the things that happen to you," Alondra says.

"Almost every night, there's noises," says Alice. "Doors slam. Lights turn on and off. Most of it is while we sleep. Usually after midnight. One night, a window shattered. I've seen black tar-like footprints in Kyle's study that disappeared the next day. And I clean Kyle's study daily. I've been doing that for years, even before he died. Thick dust settles on the desk every morning. No matter how many times I clean it, the dust settles again. But I feel compelled to clean it daily anyway to get rid of the ghost."

"She showed us, Alondra," says Raymond. "We saw the surface wiped clean yesterday. I'll show you upstairs."

"Kyle is your late husband?" Alondra asks Alice.

She nods.

"Most of the activity is in his study," David says.

Alondra nods. "Anything else?"

"Screams," says Maybelle. "Howls that sound more like monsters than wind or any animal. Terrible sounds accompanied by objects being thrown or dropped."

"Poltergeists," Alondra says, cocking her head and nodding to David.

"You've gotta see this shit." David laughs. "It's fucking amazing." Then he puts his hand over his mouth, looking at the mom and daughter. "It's incredible. I'm gonna record all I can, if that's all right."

"As long as you don't record me."

"What about him?" David gestures to me.

"He's not a witch," Alondra says with a chuckle. "It's fine with me if it's fine with Lee."

"I don't care," I say.

"You might end up on television." Alondra laughs. "Ray over there has dreams of selling a movie."

"I can only dream," Raymond says with a laugh.

Alondra pats Alice's shoulder. Then she gets up and walks over to me. "Liam, you can stay down here with Alice, if you want. But you keep telling me you want to see magic. Maybe if you see enough, you'll finally believe."

"But you said that a poltergeist could just be Maybelle being psychic."

"Isn't psychic energy magical?" Her grin is too wide.

Alondra nods and turns back to Alice and Maybelle. "We'll be right back. I have to feel this place. Okay?"

They nod.

We follow Raymond and David upstairs. Again, though everything is bright, it seems dim. Worse, the lights along the stairwell flicker as we walk up the steps. Then Alondra freaks me out more by putting her hood over her head.

"What are you doing?" I whisper to Alondra.

"Scaring ghosts. Why are you whispering?"

Raymond and David laugh.

"We're just playing with you, Lee," she says with a laugh.

"But you didn't take your hood down."

"No, I'm serious about that. Believe it or not, ghosts can get scared too."

"You stick around this witch long enough, bub," says David, pulling something out of his pocket. "I tell you. I'm telling you, you won't believe your fucking eyes and ears."

The hallway gets darker.

Ray presses some buttons on his camcorder. Then David

walks in front of him with this weird beeping handheld device.

"Which room?" Alondra asks.

Raymond points to a closed door to the right.

"It was used as his study," Raymond says. "Kyle was an architect." As Raymond holds whatever thing he has in his hand close to the door, the beeps go crazy. It reminds me of a Geiger counter.

"You want to open the door?" Alondra asks me with a smirk, like a total bitch. I roll my eyes.

"It's going nuts," Alondra says, staring down at the machine. "Wow."

"What is that?" I ask.

"An EMF detector," Alondra says. "It detects the electromagnetic waves I was talking about downstairs. These energies are common around spirit hauntings."

Alondra puts her palm on the white wooden door. Then she closes her eyes. She stands like this long enough to really creep me out.

I shiver. At first, I think it's because I'm creeped out. But it actually feels icy cold. Then I fall against Alondra. I was pushed. I'm sure someone shoved me, but all three of them are in front of me.

"What's wrong?" Alondra asks, cocking her head.

"Someone pushed me."

"Um-hmm," she says with a smile, resuming touching the door.

"What are you doing?" I ask.

"Alondra doesn't need an EMF detector, man," David says. "She can feel the energy."

Then Alondra loses her smile. She takes her hood off and cracks open the door.

"Kyle?" she asks. "Kyle, are you here? Come out so we can see you."

There's a flash of light. It's David shooting pictures with his Polaroid camera.

The room is very dark. The only light is from Ray's camcorder bulb. I see the desk by the window. This must be the desk Alice was talking about. I'm glad I don't see some sort of spirit sitting in the chair. There's a window too, but it's dirty and too foggy outside to see much of anything.

Alondra weirds me out more by standing in the center of the room, closing her eyes, and sticking her palms out. She takes a deep breath.

The EMF detector beeps like crazy.

There's a scream. It sounds like it's from downstairs. Alondra doesn't turn, but the two ghost hunters do.

"I'll go see what's wrong," I say.

"No, Lee," Alondra says with her hands still out. "Stay here. It's the ghost. It's not Alice or the girl. He's downstairs now."

Then she walks to the desk and runs a finger along the surface. She presents her index finger to us with a big smile. Ray shines his camcorder light on her hand and there's, in fact, a film of dust.

"Alice cleans this every morning," Ray says with a nod. His smirk mirrors Alondra's, and I really want them all to stop being so excited about all this.

"Come here, Lee," Alondra says. "Alice comes into the room every morning and cleans it. Our friends here saw her clean it. The ghost then makes a mess again. It's the first thing that spooked poor Alice."

"It's just dust," I say.

"Flash the camera light over the desk," Alondra says. He shines the light, and the surface, in fact, has a film of dirt. "Liam, what causes a desk to become dusty after being wiped every day? Ray, do you have the footage from yesterday?"

"It's the real deal, Alondra," he says. "I told you."

"Yes. I feel that. I'll look at the pictures later. Of course, there is fake dust. But I doubt this is being staged by Alice or Maybelle. You all met them. They're horrified." Alondra walks over to a cabinet and takes out some books. They're notebooks with handwritten documents. "Alice should have gotten rid of all his stuff. This room is keeping a trace of his past."

There's a crash. It sounds like a bookcase, or something, was turned over downstairs. Then we hear dishes breaking and Alice—this time I'm quite sure it's Alice who screams.

Alondra turns to us, her green eyes wide under the camcorder light.

We all rush down the flickering stairway. On the living room couch, Alice is holding Maybelle, crying. Alondra walks over to her and sits beside them again. She puts a hand on her back.

"It's all right," Alondra says.

"I can't take it anymore," Alice cries. "It has to stop!"

Alice points towards the kitchen. I walk around the wall and see a bunch of dishes shattered on the tile floor. Some are on the carpet of the living room, apparently thrown all the way from the kitchen. The refrigerator has been pulled completely from the wall and is leaning against the counter.

"Did you see what you were looking for?" asks Alice. "Can you get rid of the ghost? Can you help us?"

Alondra nods slowly, but she seems hesitant.

"Can you help us?" asks Maybelle.

"He's a wily ghost," Alondra says. "I tried to draw him into the room upstairs and he rushed down and attacked you. I think you should leave this house. The paranormal energy is too powerful."

"We don't have the money to move," Alice says, shaking

her head. "I can't take Maybelle anywhere else. And who'll buy a haunted house?"

"I can get rid of the poltergeist. I can absorb its energy. But I warn you, it will likely only be temporary. He can, and probably will, come back if you don't leave."

"You're saying *he*," says Alice. "Is it Kyle?"

"No. Your husband passed to the Summerland. But his passing has awoken the energy I spoke of and brought someone else. You said the house is old."

Alice nods.

"Mom, look!" Maybelle cries.

On the coffee table, Alondra's cup of tea is shaking.

"Holy shit!" cries Ray. He scrambles for his equipment, throwing his camcorder over his shoulder, and turns on the light again. I can't believe my eyes. The cup is rattling by itself on the wooden table.

"Turn the vid off, Ray," Alondra demands, jumping up. Maybelle's crying hysterically now in Alice's arms. When Ray keeps pointing the camcorder at the coffee table, Alondra shouts at him, "*Turn it off!*"

The video camera bulb cracks, and the light goes out. "Alondra, why would—"

"*Prohibe*," Alondra says, running her arm over the entire coffee table. The cups stop shaking. Maybelle stops crying. Then the young girl stares at Alondra.

"I can exorcise the spirit, but it will be back," Alondra says, sitting on the couch between them. She puts a hand on Alice's shoulder. Alice is shaking. "You're going to have to move out of your home."

"Please help us," Alice says. "Please. Just do what you can."

Alondra looks down for a moment. Then she looks at me and nods. "All right. I'll need to use your phone."

"Alondra, damn it, that was a dirty trick," Raymond says.

"You gonna pay for a new one? Why can't you just let us record you?"

Alondra permits a slight smile. Then she turns to me. "Lee, I have to talk with you alone for a second."

We walk to the foyer and stand by the base of the stairway. My hands are shaking. I look down and squeeze my fists.

"You okay?" she asks, furrowing her brow. She holds my shaking hands. Then she smiles and searches my eyes.

"No," I say.

"Oh, the teacup," she says with a chuckle.

Uh, yeah...

"That was better than dust, wasn't it? Listen, I didn't think this house was a real haunt. Honestly, I thought we'd visit, meet my friends, and then go into Macon for dinner and go home. Now I see this home is really haunted. I want to help Alice and Maybelle. But in order to do that, I'm gonna have to hold a séance in her backyard."

"Okay."

She shakes her head. "You don't understand. I need you to go home."

"Why?"

"You can pick me up tomorrow. You don't need to see any more. It's going to get weird with my friends."

"Allie, everything about you is weird."

"I know. But..." She bites her lip and gazes back toward the living room. "I'm not going to be myself." She grabs me in an embrace and leans her head on my shoulder for a moment. Then she squeezes me and says, "If you want, you can stay, babe, but you must promise to stay indoors and keep away from the backyard. I'm going to use black cherries. I won't be able to speak with you normally. I won't be myself. We can drive back home tomorrow morning after the ceremony wears off. But, if you stay, you have to stay inside the house. You'll be forbidden to come outside with us."

"We'll leave tomorrow morning?"

"Aha. I have to use black cherries."

"Blackberries?"

"Some weekend, huh?" asks Alondra, shaking her head and looking away. "I'll make it up to you. I promise. Anyway, you wanted me to show you magic, right?"

"I saw the teacup."

"Witchcraft is cool, huh?" she says with a big smile. Then she kisses my lips. "You're a good sport."

Bentmont is not far from Hawthorne, so it's not difficult for Alondra to gather her clan. Alondra assigns me the role of door greeter, and I can't help but feel like I'm opening the door for a goth party. As Alondra's black-cloaked friends pile into the house, they act as if I'm the host. I think some even think that I'm a member of Alice's family. I am, after all, wearing "normal" clothes.

I always wondered when I'd finally meet Alondra's friends. I didn't expect it to be like this.

"I'm Jessica."

"Cass."

"Gloria."

I'm really bad with names, but I do my best at trying to remember all of the girls as they enter the home.

"Hi, Lee," says Jane, giving me a hug. She's wearing a black witch cloak with makeup like Alondra. "You're brave to be hanging with Allie at one of her haunts."

"She tricked me into it."

"Of course she did," Jane says with a shrug. "She's Alondra."

"She wanted to show me magic."

Jane raises her brow and nods. "Did she?"

I nod.

"I'm Holly, Liam," interrupts a bald Asian girl with a nose ring and multiple ear piercings. "Are you a history major, like the high priestess?"

"Psychology."

"Psychology's cool," she says. "Are you in a frat?" She's looking at my button-down shirt. Honestly, she means well, but it makes me feel stupid wearing preppy clothes.

I shake my head.

Then I'm accosted by a dark-skinned girl yanking my elbow. "Hey, I remember you. You were that boy we captured that night!" My skin crawls. She's one of the girls who was high on drugs and attacked me, naked on Hilltop Bluff. "I'm Beth," she says. "You joining? It's weird to know an outsider who knows about our ghost hunts."

"Your secret is safe with me."

"Sure. Well, you're cute. That's why we grabbed—"

"Okay, Beth," Jane says. "I don't think Liam wants to rehash that night."

"Where's Alondra, Jane?" asks a tall man with an Australian accent walking through the door. He's the only man, and a large man at that. He has short hair, almost bald, and is wearing a black witch cloak too. But he's shirtless under the cloak.

"She's in the backyard," I say.

"Who are you, mate?"

"Liam."

"This is an occult meeting," he says, "not a social gathering."

"I know."

He stares at me.

"Did you bring the juice, Capper?" Jane asks.

Capper winks and shows Jane a bottle tucked under his arm. "I couldn't get everyone to come. Whatever Alondra's up to, the circle's gonna be incomplete."

"She tried to get as many as she could," Jane says.

"Can't see why she wants to help these souls," Capper says, looking around the entryway. "Looks boring." Then Capper looks down and sneers at me. "You know, man, when I lived in Jersey, I belonged to a coven that used to sacrifice unwanted babies. We'd cut the children with curved daggers, then we'd drip their blood into a goblet and pass it around. Add a few verses, in an ancient tongue, offering our souls to Lucifer, and the dark magic was..." He closes his eyes and takes a deep breath. "Intoxicating. You up for that tonight, mate?"

"Are you trying to scare me?"

"Just telling you what we did," he replies with a laugh. Then he stabs me with a finger in the chest. "Stay the fuck away from the yard, eh?"

"Leave him alone, Cap," says Jane. "You're being an asshole."

I knock his hand away from my chest. He smiles.

"I'll see you outside, Jane." Then he hugs Jane and walks off.

"Nice guy," I remark to Jane.

"He's a jerk," she says. "But you get used to him." She turns back and flashes a smile. "But how are you doing? How are you holding up? I'm used to Allie and her ways, ever since we were little. It's all new for you."

"I'm fine."

"Well, Cap might be a creep, but he's right. Stay indoors while we perform the séance. We can't protect you, and we won't be right in the head."

"Alondra said something about blackberries. So what?"

"Black cherries," Jane says, shaking her head and laughing. "Not blackberries. Witch's berries. Nightshade. It's poison, Liam. It helps witches reach altered states. She'll use it to rid the house of this ghost."

"Why don't you guys just try beer?"

Jane laughs again. "You're funny, Lee. Nightshade is a hallucinogen. It makes us see things. But it also heightens our magic and could cause things that affect the minds of people around us too. Even if you don't partake, you'll see things if you go out there. That's why Cap is telling you to stay away. Don't come outside. Whatever you hear."

I nod.

Jane hugs me again. "Thanks, Liam. You're so sweet. I think Allie must really like you to bring you here."

"It was our Saturday night..." I was going to say *date*. I don't know why I was going to say that to her, but I was. I feel comfortable with Jane.

Jane leaves, making her way to all her friends congregating near the living room.

Pretty soon I feel like a wallflower. I open the door for a few more witches; then I saunter over to the living room by myself and plop back in the beat-up recliner. It might be old, but it's cushiony and comfortable. Leaning back in the chair, I can't see the kitchen past the wall. I have to admit, I've gotten up a couple of times to take a glimpse. I saw a bunch of Allie's black-robed witches stacking wood in the center of the grass. They looked spooky under the patio light because it's still foggy.

Alice and Maybelle head to sleep in a guest room down a hall by the front door. They haven't slept in their bedrooms upstairs for months, they told us. I suggested to Alondra earlier that they leave, but Alondra said she needed their energy in the house.

The ghost hunters head to their van, but I know they're watching via the surveillance equipment. Allie wouldn't let them record her coven outside. That would give them footage of the witchcraft she's so protective about keeping secret.

A few sheets are given to me for the couch, but I don't lie there. I'm too uneasy to sleep.

6

———

WHIRLING

I wake up from a restless sleep in my recliner. It's dark and quiet, but something jarred me. All the lights are off in the house, and I'm the only one in the living room, having resigned myself to sleeping alone while the witches are conjuring outside. I never bothered to lie on the couch. Now I don't know what woke me.

"Liam!" Someone screams. "Liam!"

I jump up, hunched over, and hobble a few tired steps around the corner toward the kitchen. Then I stop. I remember their warning.

"Liam!"

There's a bizarre array of multicolored swirling lights coming from the outside patio shining through the kitchen glass door. That makes me curious as hell. I rub my eyes and creep a bit farther. But I jerk back from another scream. Curiosity gets the better of me, and I approach the glass door.

I can't believe my eyes. Outside in the patio, figures are spinning in circles at immense speeds, like colorful, whirling bright lights, around a big violet bonfire. Light radiates from each figure: red, yellow, and green flashes of light. I shield my eyes, it's so bright. With a hand over my forehead, I squint and strain my eyes. The multicolored lights are spinning so fast, and the bodies inside them seem to be turning in slow motion. All are naked; all are women, except one male. Probably Capper, but I can't make him out for sure.

"Liam!"

There's a crash. Then I hear another scream. This one is behind me. But even as I turn, peering into the now pitch-black house, the flashing lights are surrounding me.

"*Adramelch! Beleth! Marduk! Paimon! Balam! Belial!*"

It's Allie's voice, but I can't see her. The words swirl around me.

"*Spiritus. Spiritus. Hear me! Close eyes from light and retreat from darkness. Blessed be, Hecate, holy mother, honor this vessel no more. Turn to my coven spirit of nyx. Relinquish your hold over the girl in exchange for my vessel. Those who look upon manere, I call upon Escoba to shine the light of my coven under the blessed rays of Selene. Satanus. Vessel to vessel. Maybelle to Owl-Jay. Exitus, exitus, exitus!*"

In unison, all the witches repeat: "*Exitus, exitus, exitus.*"

The floor shakes a little as if in an earthquake. A kitchen cabinet opens slowly beside me in the shadows. Slowly, metal utensils, one by one, creep down the side of the cabinet, as if held by a magnet, and then clink gently along the tile floor. The bizarre thing is they fall very slowly. They move like water from a faucet, but then the metal vibrates on the tile floor. Their movement makes me pinch my arm. I'm seriously thinking I'm dreaming.

When I return to the living room, I jump. Maybelle's on the sofa with her head in her hands, being held by her mom, sobbing. David is using a bulb from his camcorder to light the room. He can't turn the light switch on, because the witches forbade turning on light switches in the house tonight.

"What are they doing out there?" I ask, plopping myself back on the recliner.

"What they told you they'd do," Raymond says, looking down and rubbing his eyes. He seems freaked out, and that *really* freaks me out. "Stay away from the door."

"Adramelch! Beleth..."

I hear the chant. Alondra says the names and her entire mantra all over again. All the words are repeated, and they seem to spin in my head, making me dizzy. It's not loud and I wonder, if I hadn't heard my name shouted, if I would have woken up. But something woke Maybelle too.

"Close eyes from light and retreat—"

"*No!*" cries a voice again. "Liam, help me!"

I recognize it now. The voice is Jane. She sounds hurt. I hear the glass door of the kitchen being thrown open. I jump up.

"Liam," warns Raymond, shaking his head, "stay back! They said stay away."

"It's Jane," I say. "She sounds hurt."

I approach the glass door again. A naked woman, wet and shivering, with lips quivering and eyelids twitching, is lying on the tile floor. Her pale skin is glowing from the twirling lights outside. I recognize her short blond hair. It's Jane.

"Lee," she says in a broken, shaky voice. "Lee. Help me, please."

I fall on my knees beside her. She clamors for my arms in an embrace, crying. I gently lift her head. Her eyeliner is running under her teary eyes. She falls back into my arms, shivering. She's icy cold to the touch.

"Help, please."

"What's wrong?"

"Everything," she says, shaking her head. "All of it. God, every part of it. Keep her away from me."

"*Exite. Exite. Exite.*" All the witches outside are chanting the words in unison. It feels like they're referring to us now. "*Cast out the specter from nyx.*"

Jane raises her head over me, looking fearfully back at the open door. I hear rain. I didn't notice rain, but now it's pouring outside. But the downpour hasn't doused the swirling light. Jane leans on her side, staring at the door. Then her eyes open wide in fear.

At the threshold, being lit by the continued array of swirling colored lights, is Alondra. Allie's naked under her black witch cloak, but her hood is over her head. But no, she's changed... her eyes have changed from lovely green to all-white. And her eyelids and lips are twitching. This isn't Alondra. This looks like some kind of demon.

I hear a strange noise. It's like a humming machine, spinning and spinning, getting louder in my ears. It feels as if it's trying to distract me from the vision before me.

"Come back to the circle, Owl-Jay," commands the demon by the door. She doesn't even sound like Alondra. "Now. Come back and leave the outsider."

"*He's your outsider!*" cries Jane. She sits up and violently shakes her head. "You brought him! I won't, Allie! I won't! I can't do this with you anymore!"

The spinning noise gets louder, hurting my ears. I have to let go of Jane to cover them. I'm not sure where it's coming from, but it's becoming unbearable.

"Return now." Alondra's words seem to be mostly in my mind, fighting with the ever-louder machine noise. I don't see her even move her black lips. She just glares at us. "I order you, Owl-Jay."

I hear a series of frantic screams from a girl behind me. It's Maybelle. The girl's shaking in the darkness behind me, staring at Alondra. She's freaking out and I hear her mother trying to console her in the shadows, but Alice is sobbing too. Then both of them are quickly grabbed from behind and, for a moment, that freaks me out because I think it's the ghost. It's not. I see Raymond.

"Stay away from the door!" Raymond cries. "All of you! Get back. Leave her, Liam! The witches commanded it."

I wonder if he even came close enough to see Jane lying naked beside me on the floor. Or Alondra possessed, staring from the door?

I clutch my head trying to drive the noise out. My head's pounding and my ears feel like they're going to explode. I want to escape. Get out. But that would leave Jane alone.

"Return to the circle, Owl-Jay," Alondra repeats. "Now."

"*No!*" Jane screams at her. "*No!*"

The multicolored lights continue to swirl.

Alondra turns around and nonchalantly walks back to the twirling colored lights in the backyard.

Jane slides along the floor. She reaches for me, and I withstand the pounding noise for a moment, but her fingers slip from my grasp. Then she's violently flipped on her stomach by an invisible force. Jane desperately reaches her hand out for me, again, by the threshold, but I can't reach it in time. She's suddenly jettisoned out the door as if from a plane.

Alondra returns to the circle, raising her arms, with her back turned to Jane. Surrounding her are the swirling lights of her witches. But Jane hasn't rejoined them. She's kneeling and weeping as the rest of the witches continue to twirl in brilliant lights around the fire.

The machinery noise is intolerable. The sound mixed with the rotating colors makes me feel sick.

Venite. Venite. Owl-Jay.

"*Liam!*"

Alondra turns her head and stares right at me with those white eyes. I black out for a moment in pain. Maybelle screams hysterically from the other room. Then I hear Jane crying. I open my eyes and meet the gaze of the eerie pearly whites of whoever or whatever has possessed Allie. All around me I hear the words spinning over and over, *"Exite, exite, exite."*

7

THE GOOD WITCH

IN A DARK CORNER IN THE UGLY THREE-STORY BUILDING WE call the Taylor Library lies a secret enclave known only to me and a select few nerds matriculating through Hawthorne U. You have to make your way through a maze of bookshelves until you arrive at the sunken-down pit. There you'll find three recliners and a couch by a very small window in a dark corner. It's perfectly private even during this time of year, when students actually start studying.

I'm sitting alone in one of the brown leather recliners, with dim lights overhead, studying my textbook. That's when I notice small pieces of white paper floating down like snow onto my page. Then comes more. I look up and my girlfriend is standing over me, holding two books under her arm and letting torn paper spill over my book. Her long black hair is fixed in a ponytail, and she's wearing a black button-down with a checkered skirt and black leggings. She's makeup-less. Even her lips are red. The getup would almost be preppy, if it weren't so black.

I shouldn't be that surprised to find her. See, she's one of the nerds who knows about my secret spot. And she's got a big irritating grimace.

I glower at her. I'm really pissed. She pouts.

Then I look back down at my book and ignore her. She grunts.

"Found you."

I lift an eyebrow. I sigh, shake my head, and turn to the next page.

She walks over to the recliner across from me and tries to slide it over. This is really funny because the chair must weigh, like, a thousand pounds. She sighs and gives up. Then she comes back over and sits on the couch beside me, but a bit too far—which I like—and heaves a big sigh.

"Sorry, Liam," she says. "Didn't mean to disturb your studying."

"I'm not mad about that."

"Oh... good." Then she irritatingly puts one of her books to the side on the couch and opens the other one. She scoots back, pulls out a highlighter from her purse, and starts studying, as if we planned to study here together all along.

I look at her, but she doesn't look up from her book. She just says, "Hi."

"What are you doing?"

"Studying," she says with a shrug, staring at her textbook.

I get up.

She grunts again, thinking I'm leaving, I suppose.

"I'm mad that you two didn't say a damn word about what happened last night the whole drive home," I confess, falling back in my chair. "When I awoke in the morning, dazed like last time, Jane was back to being your best friend and yapping with you about clothes and the newest fucking movie that just hit theaters. Why? You never explained anything. It was like Hilltop Bluff. I woke up to you telling Alice that the ghost was gone and all was well."

"It was."

"Jane fell into my arms terrified as if needing protection," I say, shaking my head. "Protection from *you*."

"Maybe you dreamed that?" Alondra quips. She laughs at my expression. I don't. She seems like she's in a really good mood, which actually upsets me more. "Oh, come on, Lee, Jane and I have had our differences. We fight and we make up. We made up. It happens all the time. Now it's over. I heard her argument and I agreed. I won't do that to her again."

"What did you do to her?"

"Well..." She stops because, right then, a student with glasses and a backpack walks down the steps. She puts down a Styrofoam cup on an adjacent table, takes off her bag, pulls out a bunch of books, and sits on a recliner across from us.

Alondra shakes her head and leans over the arm of the couch, saying quietly, "Why don't we go to my house and I'll tell you?"

"Not this time. I think I'd rather not go to your house again."

"How 'bout your place?"

We've never done that before. She never comes to my dorm room at night. It's like it's not good enough for her. That's fine. I love her house but, boy, she must be really desperate to hash things out to do that.

She looks at my book. "Whatcha reading?"

"Something you'd be familiar with."

"Tell me?"

"Abnormal psychology."

She scowls. That makes me finally laugh.

"I knew I could get you to smile," she says. "Friends? You seemed really quiet in the car."

"Why were your eyes white last night?"

She glances at the other girl in the room. I don't relent. I repeat, in a forced whisper, "Why were your eyes white, Allie? That freaked the shit out of me. And Maybelle and Alice. I think they were more afraid of you than the ghosts."

"That was the plan," Alondra says under her breath sternly.

"What do you mean? What plan?"

"Not here," Alondra says, shaking her head and looking over at the other student. Right then, the girl looks up from her book. She sighs, gets up, piles her books in her bag, and leaves. Either she thought we were too loud or too private.

"Coast is clear," I say with a gesture for her to continue. "Now tell me."

Alondra walks over and kneels by my chair. Then she takes my hand and whispers, "Jane's mad because I used the upside-down pentacle."

"The what?"

"Remember the pentagram? A pentacle is essentially a pentagram, but with the five points encircled. We used the backwards pentacle. See, demons are a very powerful kind of magic. I used Escoba's old grimoire to call on ancient satanic demons to scare the shit out of Maybelle and her poltergeist. And it worked. It scared her. It scared her ghost. And it scared you too, right? Only..." Alondra bites her lip. "It scared Jane. Jane was the focal point. I should have used Capper, but Jane has more experience. I trusted her more. I was right to. 'Cause it worked. You didn't see any ghosts during our ceremony, right? But the transfer to her...it messed with her head." She looks back up to me and forces a smile. Then she runs her fingers along my bangs. I snatch her hand and push it away. "Just like it messed with yours, babe."

"I wasn't right in my head?"

"Some of what you saw didn't happen."

"The fight between you and her?"

"That happened."

I fold my arms and lean back in my chair. Then I look down into her eyes, pissed. "Did you slip me—"

"No, ah-ight," she snaps, standing up. "We've covered this already. I don't give things to people without their permission."

"Then what?"

She looks around the room again. It's still just her and me, but in front of me are library shelves. It's quite possible students are among those rows. I know Allie's thinking that 'cause she's looking there too.

"Why were your eyes white, Allie? Answer me. Was that a hallucination? The dusty desk, the teacup, all that was nothing compared to you. The way you looked scared the shit out of me. Did you stand by the door with white eyes, or was that not real?"

"Magic can change your eyes. Just as death does. I'm goth, Liam. The color of your eyes whitens when you die."

That makes me close my eyes and shake my head. I think I want to shake off that thought. "So you were, like... dead?"

"No, I'm a witch. I'm always dead. And very much alive."

She returns to the couch and gathers her books. Then she tucks them under her arm and heads for the steps.

"Wait. Where are you going?"

"I found you and told you what happened. Mission accomplished."

This is so Alondra. She said what she came to say, and now she's over it. I either accept it or I don't. Just like our first meeting at her house. After she told me she was a witch and pleaded her case, she was over it then too. So, just like then, there's no point in her conceited, omnipotent self spending another second discussing it with me.

"So that's it?" I ask, real pissed. "You tell me your side and then go? *Mission accomplished.*"

"I'm going back home to fix a few more things between Jane and me." She halts at the steps and furrows her brow at me. Then she sighs, shakes her head, and takes a knee by me again. "Lee, I owe you a night of heavy nerddom, alone, after taking up your whole weekend, ah-ight? I'm just glad I thought to stake out your favorite hiding place to find you."

"So everything's not better with Jane?"

"We're fine."

"And us? How about our fight? Everything's better? According to you, apparently, it is."

"Yeah, we're not fighting," she says with a chuckle. "Or maybe we are? You tell me." She leans forward puckering her lips to kiss mine. But I turn from her. She pecks my cheek. "Don't be mad, Lee. I'll make it up to you next weekend."

"You're a bad witch."

"I'm a good witch, babe." Then she blows me a kiss as she makes her way back up the steps. "I'll see you in our psycho killer study group tomorrow."

8

______

HER BOYFRIEND

WELL, SHE PROMISED SHE'D MAKE IT UP TO ME. SO I'VE BEEN excited all week about our plans to go to the mall in Atlanta for the craft show. It's Thanksgiving break, which at Hawthorne U is two weeks. Thankfully, we drive her Audi because it is snowy outside. My old eight-cylinder car is not very snow-friendly.

When we enter the sliding glass doors of the mall, Alondra's rushed by a girl in a large fake-fur coat and short blond hair. Jane. It's the exact same coat Alondra's wearing. Not only am I surprised at seeing Jane; I'm surprised by a toddler in a thick white coat holding her hand.

"Hi, Lee," Jane says excitedly and gives me a hug. "You guys," Jane says with a big grin, "meet my niece Madison."

Madison waves her small hand. Alondra giggles. Then Alondra gets down on her knees and puts her hand out to the little girl. "Hi, Maddie."

"Hi," Madison squeaks. But she backs away from her hand.

"Madison," Jane corrects Alondra.

"Maddie sounds better," Alondra says with a shrug.

Then Alondra turns to me. "Surprise!" Alondra has a stupid guilty expression. She turns back to Jane, whispering, but loud enough for me to hear, "I told him it was a craft show. Like an art show. I didn't want to scare him about your niece."

"No problem," I say with a chuckle.

"You don't mind the little tyke?" Alondra asks.

"Finger paint?" Madison asks.

"In a moment, dear," Jane says, touching her nose. "I hope they have finger paint. I really do. I know you love that."

"She's adorable, Jane," I say.

"Oh, thanks, Lee. Don't you just love her?" Jane asks. "The show's somewhere around here." Jane squints and looks all around her. "I think it's near pictures with Santa."

"Santa?" I ask. "It's not even Thanksgiving yet."

Jane shrugs.

I'm really struck by the Christmas decorations. In Hawthorne, everyone ignores Christmas. Not in Atlanta. Even though it's Thanksgiving break, there are Christmas lights and signs advertising Christmas sales in every shop window. And with a cold spell unusually early this year, everyone, including me, is wearing gloves and a long coat.

We pass the "Picture with Santa" spot. There's a line of kids, but there are no kids' crafts there. Alondra, forward as always, asks one of the elves, and we're told it's at the opposite side of the mall.

"So, do you know what you want for Christmas, Maddie?" I ask as we walk by the mall windows. Jane is carrying Madison in her arms.

"Don't know," Madison says. "Doll?" she asks looking at me.

"It's up to you," I say with a laugh.

I catch Alondra whispering something in Jane's ear.

"What?" Madison asks me.

"Did your mommy and daddy hint at anything?"

"No."

"But you're excited, aren't you, Madison?" Jane asks.

"Yep." And the girl claps adorably.

The craft show is impressive. There are like twenty tables of stuff to do and ten kids surrounding each table. Madison seems more interested in charging at other kids and breaking their artwork than actually doing any "art" herself. But she loves it.

Jane's right about her loving finger painting. Madison goes crazy messing up her fingers and face with the stuff. After half an hour, I'm exhausted. And, thankfully, Madison looks petered out too. We head back.

We pass a Victoria's Secret on our way out, and Alondra flashes me a sly smile. Then she whispers in Jane's ear again.

"I've got to change Madison, guys," Jane says. "And it's getting late. I'm gonna take her home to Mom and Dad. I'll meet you two back in Hawthorne. Okay?"

"Be careful on the drive home," I say.

"Bye, Maddie," Alondra says.

"Bye, bye," Madison says. Then she looks at me. "Bye, bye."

Alondra and I watch Jane and her niece make their way down an escalator and through double glass doors. Then Alondra hooks her arm in mine and tugs me into Victoria's Secret. "Come on. I need your help in buying something for you."

"For me?"

"I owe you. God, you were so nice to Madison. You're so nice, it kills me."

Inside she walks over to a table and sifts through some burgundy and black undies. "So what do you want to see me in?"

"What do you mean?" I ask with a smirk.

"What do you want me to try on for you?" she asks, blinking stupidly over the panty table.

"It's not like you can try it on in the store here, Allie."

She raises a finger, "Ah, but I can when we get home."

"So... you're like my girlfriend now?"

She furrows her brow. "What's a girlfriend?"

I fold my arms. She's smiling as she runs her fingers through more panties. She throws her hair back and asks, "Tell me...how many boyfriends and girlfriends get married?"

"Not many."

"Um-hmm. And how many that get married stay married?"

"Not many."

"But how many boyfriends and girlfriends fuck?"

I look around the store, and that makes her laugh hard. She shakes her head.

"And let's look at the word, shall we, Lee?" she asks, still laughing. "Not that one. The word boy-*friend*. Well, you're a boy and you're my friend, aren't you?"

I don't say anything. I don't even nod. I've learned over the last couple of weeks that she does this Socratic method shit on occasion when trying to be cute and playful. I'm tired and not in the mood.

"And I love you, Lee. Sure. I love it when I make your face red. I love it when I get you all nervous when I hug you and peck your cheek. And...you love *me,* right?" After I don't answer for a while, she says, "So..." with a shrug, picking up saffron panties, "What is a boyfriend and a girlfriend? Who cares? Unless it has something to do with us *fucking*." She makes sure to say the word *fucking* really loud.

"Don't be a bitch," I say in a whisper.

"What?" Alondra asks. "Don't be a witch? What does

that mean?" She's squinting and appears to be stopping herself from bursting out laughing.

She moves to lace bras. She picks up one that's navy blue.

"Can I help you, miss?" asks an older saleswoman wearing thin glasses and a long navy-blue blouse. She folds her arms and smiles at Allie.

"Oh, you sure can," Alondra says. She grabs a black bra and presses it against her boobs. "Do you think this will look good on me?"

"That's a floral lace. Yes, it's very nice. Yes."

"Or I could go with red?" she asks and grabs a cherry-red one and puts it against her chest. Then she does the same with a dark one. "Or black?"

"You seem to like black makeup," the saleswoman says. *That's for sure.* "I think the black one fits you." *Yep.*

"What do you think, Lee," Alondra asks smugly. "You like black. It's really important that *you* like it on me."

"I think he'll like the black one a lot," the saleswoman says with a laugh.

"Yeah, I think my boyfriend will like black too."

We returned home to Hawthorne at night. The whole drive was awful as I slowly drove—I mean, really slowly—down the icy highways and then up the secluded forested hills of Hawthorne. We meant to get back early for safety, but there was an accident on the road. It's almost nine o'clock. And though no one is home at Alondra's house, all the yellow outside lights are on. One is shining on her red carriage.

We've been quiet for the last hour. I suppose I was concentrating on the road. But now, it seems a bit uncomfortable.

"What's the red carriage in the front of your house about?" I ask, parking behind it.

"Don't you just love it?" she asks with a yawn. "It's decoration."

"Expensive decoration."

She turns to me and nods, and her emerald eyes flash green from an outside light. She squeezes my hand and smiles.

"Why do your friends call you Falconsong?" I ask as I stop her car.

"That's easy. A falcon is a leader. Take a look at your ancient Egyptian history."

"Sure, professor."

She shivers and says excitedly, "Ready. We need to bolt. It's gonna be very cold."

"You really want me to stay the night?"

"Yeah. If that's all right with you?"

Honestly? I'm a little scared. Alondra is unpredictable—fun, but frightening as hell.

"Okay."

"What's the matter?" she asks, frowning. "Are you angry about Madison? Maybe I shouldn't have tricked you. Sorry about that. But I really wanted you to come with Jane and me."

"No. It's just that, Alondra, your ideas about a boyfriend are not my own. And I didn't appreciate you embarrassing me in the store."

"But we say fuck all the time. I loved how it got a rise out of you in public. Sorry. Why does it bother you so much, anyway?"

"I'm Christian. Christians believe in love and marriage. Love between a man and a woman. Not just sex. You know, girlfriends and boyfriends."

"I finally called you my boyfriend, didn't I?"

I sigh. I just know this discussion isn't going to go anywhere tonight. So instead of answering, I open my door and walk around the car shivering like crazy. Then I open her door. She leaps out and runs, sliding by her open gate.

"Careful!"

Regaining her footing, she makes it to her front door. Then she fumbles with her keys from her purse and opens it.

Inside, the house is pleasurably warm. She turns on a switch, and the incredible diamond chandelier above lights up. Then she turns on some switches in the hallway.

"Want pizza?" she asks.

"Sure."

"We can order in."

She walks into the kitchen, and I hear her dialing. Meanwhile I meander my way to the living room. For a flash, I remember people lying in the hallway drunk or drugged. That was the first time I was in this house. She invited everyone for a welcoming party the summer before my first semester, and her house was packed with intoxicated people partying or unconscious. I remember seeing her in a tight black skirt looking cute as hell. And checking me out. She kept looking at me. Only now do I understand why she and her friends were wearing black. I turn to my left and see the dining room, remembering Alondra decked in full witch costume, greeting me on our "first date." I enter the living room on the other side of the hallway.

Her living room is really modern, with an elegant stone chimney and a sofa and chairs in strange colors like fuchsia and baby blue. A large glass sliding door leads to the backyard. I recall a hundred students walking in and out of this door at her party. Now it's quiet and too dark to see the wild grassy field and the surrounding forest.

Alondra walks in the living room with another yawn and says, "We can watch a movie or something."

She takes off her sweater and is wearing just a black T-shirt and jeans. Then she walks over to the sliding door to her porch and turns on an outside light. She stares outside for a moment.

"Everything's icing. I like ice, you know. A lot of my sisters don't. They enjoy Selene around Beltane or Litha. But I like Yule. I feel like ice and snow is beautiful, you know?"

"Sure."

"Yeah."

We sit on a couch and she uses a remote on a glass coffee table to turn on a big-screen TV. There's a documentary on baseball showing. The sports channel is for me, I think. It doesn't really matter. She leans against my shoulder, and I just enjoy sitting beside her.

The pepperoni pizza comes, and we bring the box over to the coffee table. She gets me a few beers. I'm still under-age, but it doesn't matter. And I'm sure not going to remind her. She's two years older than I am.

After lots more TV, with her sleeping with her head on my shoulder, she wakes up close to midnight.

"I'm being such a bad host," she says, stretching with a yawn. "Let me make your bed."

"It's all right. I don't mind."

"It isn't," she says, shaking her head and dragging herself off the couch. "God, that drive was so boring, it killed me. Come on."

"I thought you wanted to try on your bra?"

"Oh, I could do that," she says, quickly turning, surprised. "You want to do that?"

"We left the bags in the car."

"Did you plan that?" she asks, squinting.

"I preferred having you rest on my shoulder."

"That's so sweet." She turns very serious. "Really, Liam. You're so sweet. You know, you don't have to go with me tomorrow. This one's gonna get pretty bad. My friend told me it's one of the most dangerous haunts she's ever seen. It's not just a ghost hunt. Maybe it'd be better if you make yourself at home and stay here?"

"The roads are still slick and dangerous," I say, shaking my head. "I don't want you going alone. And how is it possible to keep that part of your life out of our relationship, Allie, anyway? You're the high priestess witch of the Hawthorne coven."

She smiles and nods, but she looks unsure. Then she reaches for my hand.

She leads me down the hall to another hallway by the door. Along this hallway is the guest room. She grabs some sheets from a closet, and I help her make the bed. When she finishes, she yawns and says, "'Night, tiger. If you need anything, holler. I'll be upstairs in my bedroom."

She hobbles sluggishly toward the door, but I snatch her wrist. I turn her and she looks surprised. I kiss her tired lips. I bring her close. She runs her hand along my back and butt, grasping me tighter. I feel her boobs against my chest, and we just French kiss, making out for a while. And it's nice.

"How's that?" I ask. Her eyes are still closed, and I run my hand along her cheek.

"Umm. You sure you don't want to get the bags from the car tonight, *boyfriend*?" She smiles slyly.

"Too cold."

She yawns again and nods. Then she stares into my eyes and gets really serious. "I like you, Lee. I really do. I like you a lot."

"I like you too, Alondra."

"Goodnight, babe."

9

ALABAMA

I watch thousands of narrow tree trunks stream by my car window like toothpicks. For a second, I feel as if we're still in Hawthorne Forest. We're not. We're hundreds of miles from there. We're not only west, but south, almost as far south as Florida. The roads are free of cars because it's early in the morning and there was a bad rainstorm last night. The odd thing is the lack of conversation in my car as I drive Allie through Southern Alabama. She hasn't said a word.

Gish by Smashing Pumpkins is playing through my car speakers. Perhaps that's why she's quiet. Maybe she's listening to it?

"Geneva Forest," she says.

"Huh?"

"Geneva Forest. We're almost there." She scoots her knees up on the seat and turns to her passenger window.

"I don't like how nervous you're acting. You're not the anxious type."

"Sorry." She puts her hand on mine. "Thanks for coming." She's not wearing any eyeliner or black lipstick. It's different to not see black around her eyes. And she even chose to wear her red "Hawthorne" sweater and jeans.

"I like your car," she adds. "It's fast. You like dangerous cars and dangerous women, huh, Lee?"

"Apparently. Why are you so worried? Are you scared of the ghost?"

"No, I'm worried about the girl. I'm scared I won't be able to help her."

"You've done this before?"

"Many times," she says with a nod. "People from all over the country ask for the Hawthorne witch. I'm famous," she says with a smirk. Then she stares back at the window. "I really am. But I can't always help. And when I fail, it's not a pride thing. It's a sadness, you know. If I fail, people have no one else to turn to."

I turn back to the road. The rising sun is shining over a gorgeous view of a small lake passing us. Ice is frosted along the yellow grass over the shore.

"It's not about performing magic. Or showing people the great witch I am. It's watching the families I fail. They know I was their last chance." She turns to me with her "natural face," which I'm beginning to like, and adds, "Do you understand?"

"I guess."

"You understand everything." And she pats my hand again.

She leans back and points to a road, in a clearing, winding up a grassy hill. "It's over there."

"I thought you said you've never been here before?"

"I haven't," she says, shaking her head. "I can feel it. I feel fear. It's not only the girl. Nor even the parents or sister. It's the ghost. Don't you feel it?"

No.

"It's raw fear."

She's freaking me out. I think she knows it because she smiles smugly again. But she doesn't say anything else.

We drive up a dirt road. It worries me a little because it's icy from last night. I warned her about ice and my old Camaro, but Alondra insisted that the roads would be cleared from the storm. Don't ask me how she knew. She probably predicted the weather with her magic too.

"It's going to get weird."

I look at her as if to say *no shit*.

"No, I mean it, Lee. I mean really weird. Ghosts have a way of tapping into your mind. Terrifying you. Imagine being more afraid than you've ever been in your life. That's what it could be like. I think this is gonna be worse than Maybelle and her poltergeist. I... I hesitated in bringing you. I think it was selfish." She turns and flashes a grin as I turn the wheel and head up a windy dirt trail. "But you make me feel comfortable. And I wanted to be with you. Anyway, I probably couldn't convince you not to come with me. Right?"

"No, you couldn't."

"When the family shows me Winona's room, I want you to stay away. Don't come in her room."

"Why? I thought you wanted me there with you?"

"You're not even a warlock. You don't know any magic. Stay back. Your mere presence in the house will help me a little."

I slow the car. There's a very narrow wooden bridge over a raging river. It looks like we could fall from the weight of my car. Very slowly, we inch over the creaky wooden bridge.

When I turn another corner, in the distance, up the road, I see a modern-looking house. It's refreshing among the dark, dead marshes and dense trees. The house is painted red and white. A Ford Bronco is parked at the front, and a pickup displaying rifles is in the back. These parts, like the counties surrounding Hawthorne, are hunting grounds.

There's a shed by the house. And a small festive snowman, made of three large balls of snow, near a mailbox. It all looks very normal. But it doesn't feel normal. Alondra's right. Something feels off. The thin trees seem to be encroaching on the grounds, almost invading it. A breeze is blowing dead leaves around the driveway. The breeze is gentle, but there's something sinister about the wind, as if it's alive. And the dark clouds overhead are moving too fast.

"Do you feel it, Lee?" I stop the car. She turns off the radio. It's quiet. Too quiet. "This house *feels* haunted."

10

WINONA

Alondra and I are sitting together on a way-too-cushiony worn brown couch, in front of a coffee table, beside a nice hot fireplace. Occasionally I look at the frosted windows. It's late afternoon now and still gloomy as hell outside. Mitch and Kathy are the parents of the two little girls, and the couple is sitting across from us. Mitch is very overweight, and Kathy is almost too slender. Winona, a plump little girl, the focus of our visit, is running around with her sister Melanie. With pigtails and matching short white dresses, they look like twins. Even their faces look alike, though Melanie is younger—I'd guess around seven. That's all very normal. But it doesn't feel normal.

Alondra is thumbing through a book that looks like it's from the fifteenth century. She calls it a Book of Shadows and a grimoire, whatever that is, from some witch named Escoba Hawthorne—apparently, the witch who the school was named after. Alondra claims this book of spells and her personal diary hold an ancient incantation from Akkadia. Being that Alondra is a history major and history buff, she explained to me that Akkadians were an Assyrian people living three thousand years ago around Mesopotamia. Their empire was the ancient civilization of Sumer. Apparently, the Akkadians used to hold ancient rites dealing with ghosts and demons.

Allie is wearing her weird black mascara and a black cloak now. She told me earlier that her "normal" clothes were for her introduction to the family. She told me she didn't want to freak them out. That reminds me of how she was dressed when meeting me at our lecture after my first weird encounter. But now she's full-on goth.

Anyway, any hope of not spooking them went out the window after she buried two small figurines of Lamassu—a god she explained was from Sumerian/ Akkadian times— and said some of the weirdest shit I'd ever heard by the front door. She also enlisted my help, all afternoon, with lighting over fifty white candles and dropping sage along the walls of the house.

As she studies her book, the couple stares at me, barely saying a word. Kathy's hand is shaking. Alondra's not making it any better. Alondra's uttering these weird ancient words, again, from the book she's reading. She did this yesterday, in her house, too. She tells me she's practicing.

"Are you the witch's husband?" Mitch asks, looking at me. Alondra looks up from the book with a very amused grin. But then she's back to her book, chanting.

"No," I say. "I'm a friend."

"You a witch?" Mitch asks. He has a thick Southern drawl. I'm not used to it. Alondra doesn't have much of an accent, even though she's from these parts. She grew up in a diversified college town. Her Southern accent is probably less pronounced than my own.

"I'm just a friend."

I tap on Alondra's shoulder. "Will you stop it." She won't. "I wish you'd stop doing that," I hiss.

"Shh," she says, shooing my hand away. "Quiet."

"Do we have to wait till it gets dark?" Mitch asks. "You reckon then's when we'll see the ghost again?"

He's asking me and, of course, I have no fucking idea. Alondra's too busy chanting to answer. But it is getting dark.

"Y'all want some cookies?" asks Kathy with a grin, leaning forward and gesturing to a bowl of Nilla Wafers on the coffee table.

"No thanks," I say.

"'Course, you two are weird enough to believe us," Mitch says. "The hardest thing is explaining it to family. And friends. Worst, we can't invite anyone here anymore. Momma wants to potluck with neighbors, but we're too scared. The haunting has stopped all our socializing."

I just nod. I really don't know what to say to that.

I look over at Winona. She's playing with a doll on the carpet. She and her sister are very quiet now. Melanie is, super creepily, just standing and staring out the window. It's like she's looking for something to appear.

The doorbell rings and I jump.

"Excuse me," says Kathy.

We hear some talking at the front of the house, and I turn as another guest walks into the living room. The guest is dressed in a cloak that looks exactly like Alondra's, but this witch's cloak is forest green. She has dark skin and looks about Alondra's age. She's bald. And her eyebrows are shaven. And she's wearing a bunch of gold necklaces and bracelets.

Alondra jumps up and embraces the woman. "May you never thirst, Willow."

"Ah, you as well, Falconsong," the guest says with a smile. "May Selene bless you."

"I've told Andromeda about this house," Willow says, looking around the living room. "If we fail tonight, she can help. This is the most challenging exorcism yet. I couldn't help the girl alone, Falconsong. Hopefully, we can cleanse the house together."

"Yes." Alondra turns to me. "Lee, this is my good friend Kenosha. Her witch name is Willow. She's the head of the Selene coven in New Orleans. The Crescent City. It's the oldest coven in America. Escoba practiced voodoo arts from those parts. That's Kenosha's style."

"Escoba Hawthorne?" I ask. "The witch from your book?"

Alondra nods.

I jump up from the couch to shake Winona's hand, but Winona beats me to it. She jumps from the floor and hugs Kenosha tight. The little girl's shaking in her arms.

"It's all right, child," Kenosha says, calmly brushing her back. "Shh. It's okay." Then she looks at me. Her eyes are as hypnotic as Alondra's, but pitch black. "Are you a witch, Lee?"

I shake my head. Kenosha quickly turns to Alondra, furrowing her brow.

"Our secrets are safe with him, sister," Alondra says.

"That's not the problem. This is very dangerous... Well, if you think it's best. Are the children's rooms prepared?"

Alondra nods.

Winona finally lets Kenosha go. The poor kid has tears streaming down her face.

Kenosha walks over to Mitch. The man jumps up and takes his cap off and nods. Kenosha smiles at him. "It might be better if you and your wife leave the house this time."

"No, Mitch," snaps Kathy. "No. I have to be here for Melanie. I won't leave her alone with..." She looks at Winona in fear. "Her."

"That is well," Kenosha says. "Remain. But stay down-stairs. The things that we have to do will shake the very foundation of this home. I need all of you..." She turns to me. "Particularly you, to remain downstairs. No matter what is said or heard. The spirits know how to create bedlam. And they will. Your presence will only make things worse."

Kenosha gently pats the top of Winona's head and brings Alondra into the other room. I hear my name mentioned a few times, and Kenosha's tone does not sound conciliatory. It sounds like they're arguing with each other.

Winona runs to her mom and starts bawling.

"It's okay, Winona," says her mom. "It's all right."

"It's not!" Winona cries. "It isn't, Momma! I'm afraid. He's gonna hurt them! Auntie Kenosha is so nice. Just send her away. He's gonna hurt all of them!" Then she looks, teary eyed, at me.

The two witches return.

"It's time," Alondra says.

"Melanie," Kenosha says, reaching out. "Melanie, come with us, child."

Melanie slowly shakes her head, still staring eerily outside.

"Melanie, you must come upstairs with your sister and us," insists Alondra.

Melanie shakes her head again.

"Go with them, dear," says her mom. "You have to follow them—"

"*Fuck you!*" the little girl cries, whirling around with wild eyes. I jump. "*I won't!*" I haven't seen the girl say a word since we arrived. "*Winona pushed me! She pushed me, Momma. She pushed me down the stairs to kill me! Keep me away from that bitch or she'll hurt me!*"

The walls start shaking as if there's an earthquake. Then a gush of wind shakes the windows. The trees are bending from the sudden gale, and branches scrape against the glass. Then it starts to hail.

"*I hate you!*" screams Winona to her sister. "I can't stand you, Melanie!"

Winona runs toward her. I think she's going to strike her sister, but instead she runs around her to the window where Melanie was standing. Then Winona starts violently bashing her forehead against the glass window. Melanie turns and stands beside her, staring outside, ignoring her sister as if she's not even there.

Kathy bawls, with her head in her hands, on the couch. "Oh god." Mitch runs over and grabs Winona's head from the glass.

Alondra and Kenosha rush to the girls.

Alondra gets on her knees and says quietly to the children, "*Lux alba.*" She waves her hand over each child's head calmly. "*Lux.* Shh." Kenosha echoes it. "*Lux.* Look to the light. *Lux alba. Lux alba.*"

Then Melanie starts bashing her head against the glass too.

Kathy screams.

"*Stop it, Melanie!*" Winona screams. "*Stop doing that! They're trying to help you!*"

Then Winona falls on her knees and bursts out laughing. She's laughing hysterically. Her eyes roll back and she seems drugged. But she keeps guffawing.

"Lucifer!" cries Melanie, pointing at Alondra. "Abaddon." Her countenance is like that of an adult. "Abaddon. Abaddon. Abaddon. Go play with your cock, pussy-loving cunt bitch. Go fuck yourself in the depths of your hell!" Then she spits in Alondra's face.

Winona leans on her side and starts crying.

I run over to help Alondra, but she throws her hand up, stopping me.

"*Lux alba,*" Alondra repeats calmly to Melanie. "*Lux. Lux alba.*"

"You have no faith!" Melanie cries, squinting right into her eyes. "No belief in God! You and your sinners spend your days under the light of Satan. One day he'll drag you to hell. Devil worshipper. Let Lucifer guide you to the stygian light of everlasting damnation and sheol. You're a witch! A fucking cock-sucking witch!"

"*Shut up, Melanie!*" screams Winona, standing up. She looks like she's gonna charge her sister again. "*I hate you!*"

Kathy finally jumps from the couch to grab them, but Kenosha says, "Stay back. You promised you would not interfere."

"*Somnos,*" Alondra says calmly, waving a hand over Melanie, trying to calm her. Alondra closes her eyes tightly. It almost seems like she's trying to calm herself. "*Somnos.* Sleep now. *Somnos.*"

"*No!*" Melanie's voice turns guttural. And for a second, I think the little girl's eyes turn white, like Alondra's eyes the night of the poltergeist.

Winona starts laughing again. Then the house shakes.

"*Somnos,*" Kenosha repeats, kneeling with Alondra before the children.

"I ask that this spirit leave this child," Alondra says. "Sleep, Melanie. Sleep. Sleep now. Calm yourself and sleep now, child."

Melanie collapses onto the floor.

"*Get out of here!*" cries Winona. Then she growls. The growl echoes along the walls and sounds like a lion.

"Quick, hand me my book, Lee!" Alondra cries, pointing to the couch.

Winona growls again. She pushes Alondra, and Alondra is thrown back a few feet. My heart's pounding. I rush over and grab the book and practically throw it at her.

"*Somnos! Somnos, somnos Ekimmu requiem!*"

Alondra gets up on her knees and touches Winona on

the forehead with the book. Oddly, Winona is thrown to the ground as if Alondra struck her. She falls unconscious like Melanie.

Kenosha and Alondra lift Melanie into their arms. They approach the stairs. "She and Winona need to go to their room," Alondra says to their parents, cocking her head back. "It's inside of Winona now. I can deal with it in her room upstairs. Stay down here like we warned you."

Winona awakens and sits up, eerily staring out the window at the dark, misty backyard like Melanie was doing for the past hour.

"My god!" Kathy cries, looking up from Mitch's arms. "But how can you help? You haven't even entered her room yet!"

"We're going to try," Alondra says. She looks at me from the corner of her eye. Then she turns and she and Kenosha carry Melanie up the stairs.

"*Venite foras, Ekkimu*," Alondra calls.

Very weirdly, Winona turns from the window with a blank stare and follows them slowly up the stairs.

11

———

EKIMMU

It stopped hailing, but the wind picked up. The windows are shaking and tree branches are still scraping against the glass. Of course, the electricity is out. That's what happens in haunted houses. Right? And all hell, literally, is breaking loose upstairs. For the past hour, I've heard inhuman guttural noises mixed with animal growls, children's screams, and—a couple of times, far worse—Alondra desperately shouting out my name. That really creeped me out. It sounded like she was in pain. And that reminded me of when Jane was calling for me in Bentmont—only this time it was Alondra, the witch who's supposed to be leading this exorcism. Her cries were mixed with odd, perverse profanity coming from the children. I've also heard Alondra shouting and fighting Kenosha. It's almost as if the spirit is possessing not only the children but both witches.

The fact that I can't go up there and can only hear the bedlam is driving me crazy. I think it's driving the parents crazy too.

Pieces of the ceiling have cracked, and dust is being kicked up around the living room. And I've seen strange balls of light float outside, among the swaying trees, in the midst of the thrashing gale.

Right now, I'm nervously playing with my fingers by the fireplace. I'm not looking at the couple on the couch. I wouldn't know what to say. I think they've finally figured out that I don't know any more than they do. We're mutually ignoring each other.

I'm so worried about Alondra. She's a witch, obviously. I believe now. I get it. She's a witch. So...can I just go?

The house quakes again.

I don't want to be here.

More crashes and screams.

I really don't want to be here.

A pile of branches, or a part of a tree, crashes against the window the girls were staring at. Some of the glass cracks. That gets Mitch to finally jump up and check the window.

Then... Silence. Complete silence. The howling wind stops. The bedlam upstairs quiets. Everything stills. Kathy looks at Mitch, afraid. But again, not a word is spoken.

A green cloak rushes down the stairs. It's Kenosha. She looks exhausted.

"Can I talk to you for a moment alone, Liam?"

That sounds bad. It reminds me of when I was in the hospital once, when my mom was sick, waiting for word about her condition. I nod, jump up, and head with her into the dark kitchen. The kitchen is lit only by a few candles.

"It's quiet," I say to her. We stand near a lit candle on the kitchen counter.

"For now." Kenosha nods, looking up. "Alondra is calming the children." She's talking in a whisper. "Everyone's exhausted. The children, me, Alondra, and even the demon. It's just a break." She turns and leans against the kitchen counter. "Ghosts feed off the living. If the living are asleep, they have no power to manifest themselves, except in dreams. Dreams can be easier to deal with."

I nod as if I understand what she's saying. Then I listen to the silence. I don't like it if it's a precursor to a lot more noise.

"You recall I'm the leader of my coven in New Orleans?" she asks with a nod.

"Yes."

"She likes you, doesn't she?"

"I guess."

Kenosha smiles. "She wants to share with you our arts? That's why she brought you here?"

"No," I say, shaking my head. "I challenged her. I didn't believe she had real power. Well, she already proved herself with a ghost haunting. But this...this—"

"Hmm," she says with a chuckle. "Do you believe now?"

I nod.

"Your care for each other is getting in the way of this exorcism. The Ekimmu is using it against Alondra. It's torturing her with images of you in pain. And she, from the illusions, is believing you're hurt. It's all I can do to calm her down. And the spirit knows that if it can confuse Alondra, it can defeat us. Alondra is far more powerful than me. I'm spending more time working on her mind than I'm spending on the Ekimmu and its possession of Winona."

"It seemed Melanie was more possessed than Winona."

"Winona's the focal agent," she replies, shaking her head. "The ghost resides in Winona. I questioned the parents. Every supernatural event only occurred in the presence of Winona...but..." She takes a deep breath and pauses for a moment. "There's something else. Did Alondra tell you about Abaddon witches?"

I shake my head.

"It's a myth, of course. It's the name for evil witches.

Devil worshipping witches. Witches who've turned to only left-sided backward magic. The worst ones are known to have turned their whole covens. They work secretly. Occult. Alondra's convinced that it was an Abaddon witch that killed her parents. She doesn't buy that it was an accident or even simply a murder. That's one of the reasons she became a witch when she was a little girl. She hunts them, but neither she nor I have ever seen an Abaddon witch. And I have told her for years that her parents died a natural way.

"Liam, no one has ever seen an Abaddon witch. But Alondra keeps searching, convinced they are out there. She's not just hunting ghosts, she's hunting these Abaddon witches. And recently, she's started using left-sided magic to reveal them." She searches my eyes as if trying to read my mind. Then, as I remember the girl on the upside-down pentagram on Hilltop Bluff, she nods as if she sees the image too. "The evil witch is a myth. Between you and me, it doesn't exist. But her obsession with finding one could actually create one. Especially with Escoba's book and her power. That book contains Escoba's power. Escoba is the source of my circle's power. It gives her my coven's power as well as Hawthorne's." She hesitates to tell me more. Then she forces a smile. "Many of us believe that her obsession is causing her a great deal of pain. Specifically, it's creating manifestations like this strange demon in Winona."

"She told me she wasn't only helping to rid people's homes of ghosts," I say with a nod. "She told me she was searching for the evil that hurt her family. Yes. But what are you trying to tell me? That she's responsible for Winona and this haunting?"

"I don't know for sure. Not intentionally, of course. But the ghost residing upstairs is not a ghost. It's a devil possession. My fear is that Alondra summoned it herself, unknowingly, with left-sided magic in her search for a poltergeist. In other words, she's conjured the exact thing she's trying to hunt. Alondra and I can cleanse a house of a ghost. I have the power to do that alone. But a demon, an Ekimmu, is another thing. Even Falconsong might not have the power to rid a house of that. The best way to do it would be to harm the witch who summoned it."

Just when my mind is spinning over the possibility that this girl is telling me that the only way to stop this haunting is to hurt Alondra, I'm disturbed by a tearing sound. It sounds like wallpaper being ripped from the ceiling and walls.

"It's waking up." She shakes her head, looking up. "A demon was planted here, Liam. A demon from a witch. Alondra might have finally found her Abaddon witch—sent to her by her own power."

"So what?" I ask, sounding much more annoyed than I intended. "You have to hurt her to get rid of it?"

She slowly nods, looking up. There's a crash. The thump and bang sounds like something heavy, like a dresser, crashed down on the floor. There's a scream, but this one's from downstairs. It's Kathy. The mom's sobbing.

Kenosha is staring at the ceiling. There's another crash. It sounds like furniture has been pushed over above us. Kenosha shakes her head. Then she smiles at me, which is weird. "You like her a lot, don't you?" She nods. "So be it. We can use your love to end this. Come with me. I need your help."

I follow her down a hallway, away from the stairs, to a first-floor bedroom. The room is empty except for a bed. And it's dark, which I don't like—considering all the sounds we heard coming from upstairs. It looks creepy. But for some reason, I find myself staring into the dark room with her for a long time. And for a moment, it's oddly pleasurable, as if it's a break from the bedlam in the house.

Then there are more cries. This time it's the children. And then I hear a scream. It makes my skin crawl because it's Alondra, hollering as loud as she can, *"Lee! Lee! Oh my god, not you!"* Alondra's sobbing while crying out my name. *"Stay the fuck away from him! I warn you!"*

"My god, what's going on up there?" I ask her from the hallway. And for a moment, I feel sick, almost as if I'm going to throw up. I think the stress is so bad that it's making me nauseous.

"The spirit is entering her head," Kenosha says, grabbing my arm and pulling me faster. "Quick! I need you to come upstairs and show her that you're okay. It will break the illusion that the demon is hurting you. If she sees that you are all right, her mind will return."

I pull away from her. "But both of you said I shouldn't ever go up there! What do you mean, you want me there?"

There's another scream. Then the sound of a hundred voices crying out, suffering. The whole house shakes. And the howling wind outside is back. The windows are shaking again.

"What's going on!" cries Mitch. "I thought it was over. I have to go up to make sure they're okay."

"No, Mitch," Kathy says. "We can't—"

A hundred screams cry out from the ceiling. It's as if hell itself has opened upstairs and an entire crowd of ghouls is wailing in pain.

"I need you upstairs now," Kenosha says frantically. "Everything you see up there will be an illusion. Don't trust your eyes and ears. Alondra herself has the power to stop it. She's stronger than any of us with my coven's book. But the demon has entered her mind. Show her you're all right. Stop her with your love, and I think we can get this to end."

It's not up for discussion. Kenosha runs upstairs first.

When I hear the door open, I hear a scuffle. The children are screaming as if there's a fight. Then I'm terrified to hear Kenosha cry out in pain. I rush up behind her, but the steps are shifting, shaking, and moving from side to side. I'm not sure if it's from the magic upstairs or from the weather outside shaking the whole house. I hear another window break downstairs. The gale is terrible. It's as if there's a tornado outside.

I trip and fall. Then I push myself up and climb to the top of the stairs. In all the darkness, there's a bright light coming from the crack under the door of one of the rooms at the end of the hall. I rush there and throw open the door.

How can I explain what I see? The light from the room is so bright that I have to cover my eyes. That's similar to the last haunt. But this isn't a group of witches spinning. An area nearly the size of the house takes up the space. I know that's absolutely impossible but, somehow, it's here. And in the center of this giant chamber, bright light is turning like a slow vortex. And in this light, the two children are hovering in the air. Circling around with them are floating objects from the room: a doll house, some balls, clothes, even the bed. Kenosha is struggling, pinned like an *x* to an invisible wall. It's in a position similar to the wooden planks I saw that night when that naked girl was roped on Hilltop Bluff. She's pinned at the distance where I'd expect the walls in Winona's room to be, but I can only see fog behind her. And she's upside down.

"I'm sorry," Kenosha says in tears, staring blindly forward. "I'm so sorry, Alondra. Please, forgive me."

I don't see Alondra until I look down. In the center of this vortex is a witch crouched in her black cloak. She's sitting like an immobile onyx, curled up, with her head in her arms. She is the only thing immobile in the whole room. Allie is repeatedly reciting under her cloak: "*Spiritus. Venite foras. Spiritus. Spiritus. Venite foras.*" And under the black witch is her book.

The word *spiritus* surrounds me. I hear it uttered over and over as if by a whole group of witches. The words turn like the light vortex, echoing forward and even backward, in reverse. Meanwhile the children are yelling down at Alondra as they continue to circle in the air above. Then they cry to me too, asking anyone to help them down.

"I invoke the power of Escoba Hawthorne," Alondra says in a strangely calm, but loud, voice. "I..." Alondra lifts her head from her cloak and gazes right at me. Her eyes are pearly white.

"*You brought him here? You fucking bitch!*" Alondra turns her head to Kenosha. "*How dare you! You want to fight me!*"

"*No,*" says Kenosha, crying. "*No. Please. Forgive me, Falcon-song. Forgive me.*"

The room shakes so hard that I lose my footing and I'm thrown to the ground. Then I hear more glass shatter downstairs.

"*How dare you!*" Alondra cries. She looks up at Kenosha, still pinned backward in an *x.* "I'll tear you limb from limb! You touched him? *Damn you!*"

"*Forgive me!*" Kenosha cries. "*Please. Forgive me.*"

There's laughter, but it seems to emanate from the walls.

"Alondra," I cry. "The children! We have to help the children!"

"I told you to... " Alondra says, standing up. She turns to me with her creepy eyes. Then she points, with an extended arm, to the door.

"*FUCKING STAY OUT!*"

My body is hurled from the room. The door slams behind me.

The little girls scream.

I jump up and run to open the door again, but it's

jammed. I hear the kids screaming louder now. That gives me the strength to try for the door again. I throw my whole body at the door. Once. Twice. Then—

A hideous monster, tall, lanky, and armless, without a mouth or discernible face, is in the shadows in the center of the room facing me. It's just a dark room with four walls. A normal sized room. But this tall, thin shadow is standing in the center. The two kids are no longer flying, nor are any objects. The two children are crouched in a corner, holding each other, shaking. Kenosha, only recognizable by her forest green cloak, is standing with her back to me facing the wall, like the children facing the window earlier. Alondra is nowhere to be seen. But I hear her voice still chanting all around me: "*Venite Foras. Venite foras. Spiritus. Spiritus.*"

I run for the children. I think I run through the specter itself. I don't care, I'm desperate to help them. But when I grab for them, I lurch back. The kids are laughing at me.

"Alondra," I say to the ceiling. "Please. Help the kids. Alondra!"

"Shh... Lee, it's okay. Turn around." It's Alondra's voice. She's practically whispering.

Everything is silent—that same quiet that makes me more afraid that the noise will start again. The storm's over outside. There's not a sound.

I turn and Alondra is standing before me stark naked. Dim moonlight shines through the window on her silhouette. I didn't even notice the bedroom window before. The dim light is shining over her breasts, hips, and ass. She's alluring. Sexy. I...I can't grasp what all the excitement was about. I don't know why I was rushing. Why? Why was I rushing? Everything is calm. Everything's quiet. Pleasurable, like the calm I felt when I looked into the dark room downstairs. What could possibly be wrong? Everything's fine. And I feel as if I'm alone with Allie. My girlfriend. Her eyes are green again. And she's naked. My heart is racing, but I believe it's because I'm so excited to see her standing seductively in the nude before me...for me.

She takes my hand and strokes my fingers.

"Let's fuck in front of the children."

Winona snickers. Melanie is pushing her sister, trying to move away from her, but Winona is pulling Melanie back and pointing at us, laughing.

"What is this evil?" I ask.

"Me."

She rubs her left breast, running her fingers along her nipple, and uses the same hand to touch my cheek. "Come on, Lee. Fuck me. You like what you see, don't you? Aren't I your *girlfriend*?"

Then she takes my hand and runs it along her breast. She guides my other hand along the crack of her ass. Then she locks her lips to mine and we kiss. I'm very aroused. She strokes me and squeezes me tightly to her naked body.

"*Venite foras*," she says, looking into my eyes with a nod. "*Venite foras. Spiritus. Spiritus.* Take off your clothes. Let's fuck. Don't worry, I'll make sure to cover the children's ears. They can just watch."

No!

I push her to the ground. There are more inhuman screams. The floor moves again, and I struggle to reach the kids.

As I gather them into my arms, the two girls shake and kick, resisting me, but they're small enough for me to carry out of the room. I run as fast as I can down the stairs with them.

Mitch is right there at the bottom of the steps. He snatches them and pulls them away from the stairs. Then I hear Kathy join him. I hear a door open downstairs and more wind from outside, and then the outside door slams shut. The family's left their own house.

It's pitch black upstairs. I walk slowly back up, but I'm more afraid than ever to enter that room.

Inside Winona's room, Alondra hasn't moved. She's lying on the floor in her cloak now, but in the same position she was in after I shoved her. Kenosha is still staring, possessed, facing the wall.

"What do I have to do to expel the ghost?" I say, practically to myself, because I don't trust anyone anymore. "Please, help me, Alondra! What can I do about this storm?"

"Windstorm," Alondra says, lying on the ground, in a broken voice. She's crying. "Yes. Windstorm. This I breathe. Hawthorne witch. Wait for the next one. And leave me, Lee. It's me. It's me."

Alondra curls in a ball and cries. The ghost still must be possessing her to cause such strange behavior. But the house isn't shaking. There's no sound of wind outside. It's quiet.

I fall on my knees beside her. She quickly grabs for me. At first, I push back, afraid, but she's clutching me as if she's afraid I'll let go. She squeezes me tightly, weeping in my arms.

"I watched you die," she says in my arms. "My god, Lee, it was horrible. You, my only angel. I watched you take your last breath in my arms. And it was my fault. Then there was a group of people walking with your coffin. You left me. My angel. You left me alone."

"I'm not dead. I'm here, Allie."

"I know. Please, god, Lee, don't ever leave me again."

"That's why I brought him upstairs," Kenosha says. She's standing beside us now in the darkness.

"You shouldn't have," Alondra says, wiping her eyes on her sleeve. "No, you shouldn't have. God, Kenosha, that devil was so empty. So sad. Longing for someone but never having contact. What a terrible torment. How can anyone or anything exist like that? Only to harm others."

The lights switch on. The power is back on. And we find ourselves in a very messy but "normal" kids' room. Kenosha leans over, breathing heavily. "The wraith's left us, Falconsong."

"Thanks to Liam."

"Thanks to you," Kenosha says. "You cleansed another spirit. I brought him to make things right for you."

"It could have possessed him," Alondra says, shaking her head. "You shouldn't have done that."

"It was the only way to get you back. It's never been this hard." Kenosha sighs. "I don't think this was just a lone Ekimmu. It was like fighting an army of them. Hecate empowered this wraith, sister. Winona was the vessel. She was the talisman cursed by a witch. Perhaps an Abaddon, as you claim. It's not the house. She was cursed to draw us here. Perhaps in order to take over your mind."

"But the spirit's gone from Winona," Alondra says, nodding. "That's all that matters."

Kenosha helps Alondra up. "It came for you."

"Is it over?" I ask.

"Yes, Lee," Alondra says with a rueful grin. "Lee, I should never have brought you here. I'm so sorry. I should never have had you come."

12

ANTLERS

We're staying in a one-bedroom motel in a small town in Alabama. It was too late in the evening to drive home. I insisted on the couch, so Allie took the bed. But I've been tossing and turning. I can't stop seeing images of that tall lanky demon spirit I saw in Winona's house. I don't need to worry about having a nightmare, I lived one.

The alarm clock is ticking loudly. Yellow light is shining around the edges of the curtain by the front door. Other than that, it's dark. I close my eyes. I try to rest in the quiet. But quiet reminds me of that house. The silence always portended something terrible.

I jolt awake due to the sound of banging. My eyes open, but it's dark. The only light is still shining through the curtain from the walkway beside the parking lot. I'm thinking I see a shadow of a deer or something.

Bang. Bang. Bang.

There it is again. I squint at the window. Then I roll off the couch and walk to the door. Through a crack in the window, I see a figure. I open the curtain. It's a girl. She's crouched down beside the front door, naked, covering her breasts and groin. It's Alondra! I whirl around and see that the bed is empty. Then I throw open the door. Allie's crouched, shaking. Her mascara is running down her face, and her naked body is dripping wet.

"What happened!"

I help her inside and shut the door behind her. She won't stop shaking. I turn the light on, I squint from the brightness —though it's just dim lamp light—then I yank the sheet off the bed and wrap it around her body.

"Lost the room key," she says with chattering teeth. "Thank you. Hold me, Lee. You're warm."

I grab her tightly, but that makes me push her off me. She's frigid. She falls to the carpet, and I get on my knees beside her.

"How long have you been out there?"

She shrugs. She's so cold that her lips are blue and her teeth are chattering. I put my arm around her again, but even under the bedsheet, she feels like ice.

"It's...it's a wandering."

"A what?"

"A wandering." She attempts a smile, but her lips twitch. "A... witch wandering."

"Maybe I should take you to the hospital."

"No, I don't believe in hospitals," she snaps. "No." She takes a deep breath. Then she repeats sternly, opening her eyes wide, "No."

"What can I do?"

"Hold me... And change the temperature. God, it's so fucking cold...find the thermostat. Make it warmer."

I jump up to do that. But she grabs my wrist. "No, forget it. Just hold me. Jesus, it's so cold. Do we have anything hot to drink?"

"There's a microwave. Tea bags and a mug, I think. I can microwave some tea."

I get up even though, at first, she doesn't want to let me go. I search for a coffee maker on a shelf and find a Styrofoam cup and tea bag. Then I run to the faucet by the bathroom, but the water isn't coming out. Are the pipes frozen?

"The water's not running."

"*Fluenta!*" she cries, almost screams. Water bursts into the sink. I grab and fill the mug. Then I throw it in the microwave.

After forty seconds, I run back with the cup.

Oddly, she's taken the bedsheet off. She's in the nude again, sitting on the floor holding her knees and shivering. She turns her head to the left and right in an odd way, like a bird. Then our eyes meet. Those green eyes gaze at me. Despite her shaking, she smiles. It's a sultry grin, which is unnerving. It creeps me out, because it reminds me of the haunted house.

"Come over and warm me," she says.

My legs obey. I find myself on my knees before her again. I hand her the cup. She takes it with two hands as if it's some holy vessel. But the weirdest thing is that she stops shaking after drinking it. Then she gently puts it down beside her on the carpet. She touches my hand. Her hand is warm.

"I'm feeling better," she says with a smile. "Thanks, Lee. How about you? That was a really strange night at the house, huh?"

Ah...yeah. How about now?

I squint at her. Small talk feels really weird.

"*Fructus,*" she says earnestly with a nod, as if that's the answer. Then she picks up the teacup and drinks more tea. I catch myself staring at her boobs and she smiles. Then she runs her hand along my neck and nightshirt. "*Fructus.*"

"What? What are you talking about?"

"*Fructus,*" she replies plainly. I heard that word before. I can't place where.

She takes my hand and kisses the back of it. My eyes glance at her breasts again. She notices and I feel myself blush. I quickly look back at her face. That's worse. We lock our gaze. Those bright green mesmerizing eyes stare.

"I can't take it when you're naked," I mutter, shaking my head.

Why did I say that?

She laughs with a nod. "*Fructus. Fructus coitus.* It's *fructus.*"

She takes my hand and runs it along the curve of one breast and then over an erect nipple. Her skin isn't cold anymore. It's warm. Then she closes her eyes, brings my fingers up to her mouth, and takes a finger and sucks it up and down seductively. I yank my hand back.

"What's the matter?"

"You're freaking me out," I say. "This is like Winona's house. You were freezing a second ago."

"It's me. But I'm fighting a trance." She shuts her eyes very tight. "I think it was probably triggered by Winona. Yes. I had a witch's wandering. I felt compelled to wander outside. A wandering makes us one with nature. We become like animals. We eat like animals. Sleep like animals." She opens her eyes and stares right into mine again. Then she leans close and touches her lips to mine. Between kisses, she says, "And we...*fuck* like animals. It takes all my strength not to tear your clothes off right now."

I laugh nervously, but she nods.

"If you don't want this, I think I can stop. I know that I want you. I've been attracted to you ever since I met you."

There's an outdoor dirt smell to her skin. But her perfume smells four times stronger. She has a pumpkin-lavender smell.

She's shivering again. Somehow, I find my hand rubbing her back, trying to warm her. She scoots up a little and my fingers accidentally slip down over the crack of her ass. She snatches the hand back and kisses it.

"Leave the room if you don't want me. Even go into the bathroom for a few minutes. Leave. Or... stay with me. Hold me. But choose. I can't control this much longer."

"What kind of magic—"

"Make a choice," she says, shaking her head.

She takes a deep breath, smelling the air, as if she's taking in an exquisite aroma. Then she grabs my hand hard, running her fingers up my arm and massaging my skin. She twists my hand, hurting me a little. But then she brings my fingers to her mouth and kisses them again.

With my other hand, I pull my nightshirt over my head as an answer. Her eyes widen and her hand quickly drops mine. Her fingers glide over the sparse hairs of my bare chest and then over my stomach, running over the ridges of my abs. She locks her lips hard on mine as she continues to rub me. Her hands land between my legs.

Apparently, removing my shirt was enough. She pushes me on my back on the carpet. Then she mounts me. I'm expecting to be shocked by her cold skin, but she's warm. Her boobs hover over my face. I reach up and suck one, while running my hand over the soft curves of the other. I'm squeezing her, finally touching her body in ways I could only dream of before. She giggles. She moans as I suck. I've never done that before. Then she dips down and strokes my shoulders and neck. She reaches down again to the bulge in my underwear. Her hand glides inside and touches the skin of my hard cock. Now I know she was right. There might have been a choice before, but now it's gone. We're committed.

And yet, even now, I push her off.

"What's the matter?" she asks, amused. She's on her side on the carpet.

I run to a chair, by a desk, where my pants are hanging. I rummage through my wallet and grab a condom. It doesn't take me long to get back to the floor.

She throws back her long black hair and mounts me again on the carpet. She smiles at me. But this isn't the sweet Alondra smile; she looks hungry. And her beautiful face scares me a little in the dim lamplight. Her dark mascara is running.

She grabs my hand again and runs it along her soft skin, guiding it down her side until it finds the crack of her ass again, while joining my lips to hers painfully tightly. Then she rocks over my hard cock through my underwear. She says the words between kisses:

"*Fructus. Coitus fructus.*"

Now I remember those words. It was from the dark-skinned girl named Beth who tried to rape me on Hilltop Bluff. That memory is enough for me to want to stop again.

But Alondra yanks my underwear off and tugs it from my feet. I'm naked like her. Then her fingers, with those long black fingernails, glide over the skin of my naked, erect cock. She rubs it. She keeps rubbing it until I moan. Then she tears off the condom wrapper herself and slides the rubber over my cock. After a little bit more stroking, she lies on top of me again.

I move my head away.

"What's wrong now?" she asks, almost in a grunt. "You want me to stop? Really? What's the matter, Liam?"

"Those words are the words I heard on the hilltop."

"What words? *Coitus fructus*? It means *fuck*. It means I want to fuck you. I really want to fuck you right now. Don't you want to fuck me?" Then she adds, almost in a whisper, by my ear: "*Fructus. Coitus fructus.*"

That's irresistible. Is she casting a spell on me? Or is it just her?

"I've never done this before."

"Fuck? Or fuck a witch?" She actually laughs. I don't think it's very funny. She frowns at me.

Then she closes her eyes and grinds against my cock again. But I haven't entered her yet. She gazes down with her infamous smile. Even now, naked, she's Alondra, looking totally sure of herself. She gently runs her hand along the stubble on my cheek. That eases me a little. Then she brings up my head to hers and kisses my lips.

My heart's thumping. She's holding my head while grinding over my groin. Even her scent, the lavender perfume, seems to hold me. I desire to be close to her so much now.

"Let me translate," she says, still grinding. "Sweet. Sweet...sex. It's a..." She dips down and her lips dance with mine. I can't move. I'm frozen. I don't know if it's a spell, but I literally can't move. But I don't care. I don't want to move. "It's Latin for *sweet*. 'Sweet sex.' Or, if you prefer, *fruit*. Fruit fuck, Lee. Fucking... I can...try to stop if you want me to. Do you want me to stop?" She runs her lips down my neck and over my hard chest. "Please say you don't. Please."

Then she drags her tits along my stomach, moving her body over my cock, only arousing me more.

"Do you...want me to... stop...Lee?"

"No. Don't stop. Please don't stop, Allie."

"You really haven't had sex before?" she asks. "Are you serious?"

I nod.

She takes a deep breath over that, as if it's intoxicating, and ravenously dips down, pressing her lips hard against mine like an animal. She's breathing so hard I can feel her blow along my lips. She laughs and squeezes me so tight it almost hurts. Then she enters my mouth, running her tongue along mine.

"But those were the magic words that night," I say, between her sucking. "This isn't you. It's a spell."

"This is me, not a spell. I'm a witch, Liam. But I like you. And I would never harm you. Never. I would hurt myself before hurting you. I can't believe no one's done this with you before. You are so incredible."

I'm incredible? No, *she's* incredible.

She moans in pleasure as I enter her. She gently pushes in and out on top of me. I squeeze her breasts; then I lean forward and take her in my mouth again. She's groaning while pressing her lips and body against me. Then I find enough strength to raise myself into her. That makes her cry out more. She pumps faster. We're moving together. As we touch, I turn to my right and I swear I see the silhouette of a deer with antlers standing by the window. It nearly distracts me until—

"Take me," she says. "Don't stop."

She places my hands on the crack of her ass, now moist, bringing me closer, deeper. Then she's back at my mouth, practically chewing on my lips. I taste her tongue.

"You've never had sex before?" she asks, looking into my eyes. "Are you serious? Really?"

I hesitate, but then I nod.

"Oh, Lee. Thank you."

"Thank you? For what?"

"For sharing that. Only you would. You're so amazing."

"No, you are, Alondra."

She leans over and kisses me again, still grinding into me. Then she sits up straight over me, throws her hair back, and shakes her head. "No, you are."

The shadow of the stag is kicking and bucking like crazy by the window. I'm sure I see its shadow now. I'd point it out to Alondra if we weren't so intimate. The hooves of the animal are clopping against the walkway as its bucking up and down. It seems to be in tune with the rising and falling of Alondra's body over mine.

Alondra gently turns my head and looks deep into my eyes. She smiles as she presses into me faster. I try to turn back to the window to look at the stag, but she gently pushes my head back again. She smiles, opens her eyes wide, and stares, in the dim light, into mine. As she rocks her body inside me, she wants me to stare into those bright green eyes. Is she hypnotizing me? I don't care. I love gazing into her. Maybe she's doing it because she knows I love looking at them so much. I don't want to be anywhere else except with this girl, right now, so close. Gazing into her.

The stag is clopping loudly enough now for Alondra to finally turn and look at the window. It's jumping up and down, crazy. So is she.

She looks away from me and loses her smile.

"I'm going to cum," she says. "Oh, god, Lee! You're incredible." She grinds harder and leans down, sucking on my lip. Then she lifts her head and extends her body straight back, exposing the curves of her boobs and nipples. She throws her black hair back, moans, and falls down on me, landing on her elbows. She cradles my head, locking her eyes with mine again, so close I can feel her breath over my face. "Oh, Lee. Liam. I love you. I'm cumming! I really love you, Liam. I know it now. I love you so fucking much!"

She climaxes with me inside her. That makes me orgasm too. We fall to our sides. But then she quickly gropes for me. It reminds me of Winona's room. It's as if she's afraid I'll leave her if she doesn't grasp me in time.

She's cold again. Icy freezing cold. She's shivering and her icy body makes me shiver too. And this is like when I hugged her in the pool by her house. It's that cold pleasure. Her skin is like ice.

"Rest with me," she says with heavy eyes. "Lie with me.

I'll keep you warm, angel. You're my angel and I will care for you."

"Why were you outside in the middle of the night, Allie?"

"I'm a cold witch. But you warm me."

13

PRETZELS

I've got my backpack slung over my shoulder while chomping on a large soft pretzel as I walk down the main pathway at Hawthorne University. This thoroughfare is the main drag for everyone in school, with brick buildings and groomed trees by the side and a ton of students walking together on the wide cement path. There are also a few tents along the boulevard where they sell stuff, like these amazing Bavarian pretzels. I tell you, they freshly bake the best pretzels in the world at Hawthorne. I don't know what the hell they put in it, but it's so magically soft, crisp, and delicious. The walkway will end in a large grassy hill. And above that hill is our main library.

I won't be seeing Allie the rest of the day. She's got private witch business. I haven't told her—I haven't told anybody—but, honestly, I'm getting seriously creeped out. She's a witch. I get that. But she's also my girlfriend. I had sex with her, so she's my girlfriend now, right? I think that was her definition. I'm conflicted. Having sex made me feel on top of the world last night. But then I woke up remembering demons and ghosts.

Let's fuck. Don't worry, I'll make sure to cover the children's ears. They can just watch.

I mean, that was seriously fucked up. And it pretty much sums her up. She's an egotistical, conniving, controlling, screwed-up-in-the-head witch. Do I really want to be in love with that?

You are in love with that, Lee.

I can see her saying that to me. Yeah. And, fuck me, but wouldn't you know it, my chest rises at the thought of her saying it.

Well, today, despite my confusion, it's pleasant outside. The clouds are gone. The sky's blue. It's a bit cold, but as I get closer to the library, I see it's warm enough for many students to be lounging on the grass.

I have to study. I have a big statistics test tomorrow. I have to memorize construct, content, and criterion and validity in order to pencil in the right multiple choice answers next week. God, I hate statistics.

I take a turn and make my way to my dorm. I pull the glass door open. The hallway seems really dark after being in the bright outdoors. There are a few people rushing by, and I nod to a couple of neighbors. It's loud inside, which only makes my room seem quieter when I enter it. It's unbelievable that they still haven't found me a replacement roommate yet—not that I mind the room all to myself.

I lie on the bottom bunk, lean over, and touch the button on my answering machine.

"Call me," a voice says, and then hangs up on my answering machine. It's not Alondra, it's my friend Bill.

I reach over and grab my small white phone headset, uncoil the plastic cord, and press his number on speed dial.

"Hmm, yeah?" Bill asks on the line.

"Hey, Billy," I say, munching on the last bite of my pretzel.

"Liam? How the hell are you?"

"Great," I say with a laugh. "What's up?"

"Great? I thought you were hating your life?"

"No, things are getting better."

"Well, guess what? I'm in town for a couple months. I'm doing some research in Myrtle Beach. That's not far from you, right?"

"Only a few hundred miles."

"I'm working on the coast. I was hoping we could meet up. It'd be fun. We can chat about that incredibly hot girlfriend you keep obsessing about. I assume that's why you're feeling better. It can't be school. You never had problems in school. You're a nerd."

"You're a nerd too, Bill."

"Got that right. That's why I'm teaching at Duke."

"Where do you want to meet? Myrtle Beach? That's a state away."

"I could probably meet in Atlanta. I don't know about the middle of the woods, but if you're too busy, I can try to drive through the trees and find you. We'll sort it out. So, you're feeling better, huh? Why?"

"Alondra."

"Well, don't be jumping off a cliff after the breakup."

"I'm not so sure that's going to happen. I'm really into her. There's a connection."

"She's hot, right?"

"Yeah."

"That's all that matters."

I lie back in bed and stare up at the top bunk wondering if he's right. If he only knew how complicated things were.

There's a bunch of noise outside. People are shouting and laughing in the hallway. The walls are paper thin.

"So what brings you south?" I ask. "What sort of research?"

"Damn," he blurts out. "Lee...I can't talk now. I'm doing some ghost research on the beach. But I've gotta go. Just call me and leave a message and we'll sort things out. Can't wait to see you again, man."

Coincidentally, my older friend from high school is now a psychology graduate student at Duke—a *parapsychology* student. No, I'm not kidding. Seems something about me attracts me to these weirdos.

The minute I hang up with him, my phone rings again.

"Oh, you're there." It's Alondra's voice. And I melt at the sound of it. Yep, I'm in a crush, I told you. "I was gonna leave a message, babe. Just wanted to tell you I had a lot of fun last night. Maybe not so much fun at the haunting but...*a lot* of fun after." I'm completely silent. That makes me feel stupid. It probably makes her feel stupid too. She laughs it off. "I wanted to thank you again for coming with me to Alabama. Now I'm going into radio silence." That's what I call our Fridays. She fell in love with that expression a few weeks ago. It's when she doesn't want me talking to her because of her weird Friday witchery. "But I was hoping we could meet in the library tomorrow morning? Maybe at your secret enclave?"

"Sure. That'd be fun, Allie."

"Great... You doing okay?"

"Yeah, fine."

"Hmm. Sometimes I can't read you. How 'bout 'round ten tomorrow?"

"'Kay."

"Love ya."

"Okay..." *Uh.* "See you then, Allie."

14

ABNORMAL PERSONALITY

I'M IN A CLASSROOM TRAILER OFF THE EDGE OF CAMPUS, DEEP in the woods. It's an ugly white trailer with two large windows, metal stairs, and about twenty desks inside. The room is packed with students, some even standing in the back of the room. The class is full because it's a review for our test on Monday. We're listening to a teaching assistant named Trish. Trish is a fun, bubbly girl, with long blond hair, who entertains the hell out of me whenever she reviews depression.

As everyone's listening, I'm skimming through past notes about the Night Stalker and John Wayne Gacy for my criminology class. I'm multitasking—I have a test in that class next week too, along with a dreaded statistics exam.

Gacy was a real sick fuck who used to work as Pogo the clown while moonlighting as a murderer of little children. I have to remember the word "coulrophobia." That's the fear of clowns. The next page in my criminology class notes is Richard Ramirez, a.k.a. the Night Stalker. He used to run upstairs in the Cecil Hotel in Los Angeles naked and covered in blood. Somehow, he wasn't caught there. Too discreet, I suppose. He was satanic and tattooed a pentagram on his left palm. Sound familiar? Ah...love.

"Here is a list of the main categories of abnormal personalities," says Trish, with a too-big smile, pointing to an image from her slide projector. "You'll be tested on each one. Narcissistic personality is being in love with oneself. It comes from the Greek myth of Narcissus, who rejected his love for the nymph Echo, preferring to love his own reflection. He committed suicide and hence the gods immortalized him by their creation of the daffodil. An interesting tale. The background of the word isn't as important, just remember the personality. Next we have here..." I'm scribbling notes about daffodils while jotting down facts about killer clowns. "Schizotypal personality. These individuals act similar to people suffering from schizophrenia."

As I turn the page back for a second to glance at my notes about Gacy, I jump in my chair. There's a large red backward pentagram splashed over the page. The creepy thing is, I didn't draw it. I don't even have red ink.

I look around the room and everyone is still staring intently at Trish. And the girl sitting to my right apparently didn't see the symbol or notice me flinching. She just leans her chin on her hand and watches our TA. The guy to my left is flipping through his notebook. Where did the symbol come from? Am I losing it after Winona's haunt?

"Except these people don't see or hear things," says Trish. "You know, these people are loners engaged in magical thinking, superstitious beliefs, and paranoid thoughts. They often dress strangely."

Sounds familiar. Except Alondra is not a loner. But I've been known to keep to myself. Maybe I fit this one. No, I'm not that much of a loner.

I hear laughter. At first I think it's the student to my right, but she's busy jotting down notes. The guy to my left is staring at Trish. Then I think it's the TA, but she's pointing at a slide.

My heart beats fast. I feel nauseous. Sick. I look down and my hand holding my pen is shaking.

I feel trapped.

They all know how tough the tests next week will be. I've been busy gallivanting in haunted houses with Allie so much that I'm going to fail. This is not a hard class, you know. Not even an uninteresting one. But, god, what about my statistics class?

I can't breathe. I feel like I should get out into the fresh air.

Am I having a panic attack? I've never had one, but I think this is one. I'm ready to jump and bolt.

"Let the light of Venus be your shining light," Trish says with a nod and her bubbly grin, looking at me. She's smiley. Then she points at the projection of her diagram of personality disorders.

The room turns dark. I look at the windows and see dark clouds rushing across the sky between the trees, shadowing everything. It was clear skies before.

Enlighten. Morning. Venus. Abaddon.

I look up to the front of the classroom and Trish has disappeared. In her place are two children, Winona and Melanie, in their short white dresses and pigtails, facing each other. They're playing patty-cake, but they're not saying a word.

Shine bountiful beauty and bright. Lux alba. Lux tenebris.

It gets very dark. A pack of rats scurry under my feet between the desks. My feet lurch up and I hit the desk with my knees. I look to my right and left, but the students beside me are gone. All the seats are empty. No one's in the room except for Winona and Melanie.

My knees slam against the desk again.

"Something the matter?" Trish is staring right at me. So is everyone in the room. The stormy dark clouds are gone. The classroom is full of students. The girl to my right has her pen down, squinting. Everyone in the room is staring.

"Sorry," I mutter.

"Oh, Liam," Trish says with her sweet smile, shaking her head. It surprises me that she remembers my name. "Didn't you learn in Sunday school that the number of the beast is six, six, six?"

Satanas. Satanas. Lucifer. Six, six, six.

The words are whispered by many voices surrounding me. There's a loud crash, as if one of the desks was hurled across the room. Then the lights go out again.

Rain pours so hard that water's thrown like buckets against the windows. Clouds race again between moving branches outside.

I turn back to the front of the class. Trish is gone. So are the girls. Replacing them is a lanky armless man as tall as the ceiling without a mouth or discernible face. His white eyes are staring at me.

I look around. All the desks are empty again. Except the one beside me. Melanie and Winona are sitting next to me.

"Touched by a witch," say the children's voices in laughter. "Six, six, six. Fucked by a witch. Six, six, six. Lucifer. Lucifer. *Satanas.*" Both girls cover their mouths, snickering.

Six, six, six. Fucked by a witch. Six, six, six.

The words are repeated over and over by many voices close to my ears.

"Liam, was it fun being fucked by her? By the devil?" asks Winona, touching my arm. Her voice sounds like Alondra's.

"You're a cunt-sucking sinner, Liam," they say in unison, smiling and nodding. "Damned for all time. And guess what's going to happen to you? You're going to hell."

Six, six, six. Fucked by a witch. Six, six, six.

There's a large howl, as if all the voices surrounding me are crying out at the same time, so loudly that it hurts my ears.

"Why don't you just shut up!"

I cover my eyes, shielding them from a sudden flood of light in the room. The girl sitting beside me gasps. Those were my words. The lights are on again, it's clear outside, and Trish is standing by the slide projector staring at me like I'm nuts.

"What the hell?" someone asks.

"Talk about abnormal."

"What's the matter with him?"

"Sorry," I blurt out and quickly gather my books, jump up, and rush out of the classroom. I'm out of there. As I rush down the steps, the whole class bursts in laughter behind me.

I head back to my dorm. The sun's out and it's a beautiful day. And I'm spooked as hell. I don't know what I just saw or what's happening. Alondra will. That wasn't a hallucination, that was magic.

I'll call her.

I can't call her. We're in "radio silence."

I have to try.

15

THE OUTSIDER

A bunch of cars are parked in Alondra's driveway, some blocking each other, near her distinctive red carriage. The lights are on in the front yard, lighting her perfectly trimmed trees and freshly mowed lawn, but I don't see any lights inside the house. A breeze rustles the leaves along all the trees and the ground. I expected to hear voices but I hear nothing, only the leaves. I smell fire though. I knock at the front door a few times. No answer. So I try the side yard.

I walk along a stone-bordered path by the side of the house. That's where I finally hear voices. Alondra's voice.

"Blessings come from Hecate. Glory be the stars. Let not these clouds block Selene. And if it be, let the rays of light come in the morrow. *Lux alba.*"

"*Lux tenebris,*" says a male voice. I think it's Capper.

Through the branches, I make out a very large bonfire in the center of Alondra's backyard. Alondra has her yard neatly cared for in the front, but in the back, it's just wild grass surrounded by the tall Hawthorne Forest. And in the center of this grass, there's a bonfire. Tonight, a witch is raising her arms before the flames with a bunch of witches sitting around the fire in white plastic chairs. The central witch is Alondra, I suppose, but all I see, with her back turned to me, is her black hair and cloak.

"Tragedy's befallen one of our sisters," Alondra says, lowering her arms. "Tonight, we pray that Hecate can restore peace. Let us pray, sisters." Then, as if in church, the group chants in unison a litany: "Glory be Hecate, our supreme goddess of witchcraft. Glory be Selene shining white light under Astraeus. Let moonlight light our hearts. Gather sisters as one. Atman. Let this coven be blessed under Falconsong, your leader and high priestess of the Hawthorne coven."

I'm walking over, but everything is slowing. I don't think it's magic. I think I'm simply freaked out. Then one of the witches starts crying. That makes me feel worse. Weirder, really weirder, I hear a baby crying. I see the weeping witch crouching over a baby in her arms, bouncing her gently on her lap.

When I come closer, through the wild grass, I see the crying witch has short blond hair. It's Jane. And the baby she's holding isn't a baby at all; it's little Madison.

Alondra turns and I finally recognize her profile under her black hood. "Let us give all of our love and support to our sister, Owl-Jay," she says.

They all get up and walk over to Jane and Madison and pat her shoulder or lean down and hug her. But the toddler's inconsolable. So is Jane. That's when one of the witches sees me.

"High priestess, high priestess," she says, pointing excitedly. "Look!"

Alondra turns. They all do.

Now I've witnessed Alondra angry, but never at me. Right now, she narrows those green eyes and looks seriously pissed. She's told me a thousand times to never come to her house on Friday night. She said it's one agreement I must never break.

"What are you doing on private property?" asks the only man in the group. I recognize his Australian accent. It's that asshole Capper.

"Why are you here, Lee?" asks Alondra.

"Why is your friend witnessing our Sabbath, Alondra?" Capper asks.

"Alondra," I say, "I had to talk to you." I turn to Cap and raise a hand. "Sorry. I have to talk to her."

"These meetings are private, Liam," Alondra says, shaking her head. "I've told you that. Get out. Tell me later."

"But I have to talk to you now." I'm shaking my head. "I saw the ghost again. I think it's the same ghost—"

"An initiate is not allowed in the circle," snaps another witch. She has a nose ring under her hood. I think it's the sweet Asian girl who introduced herself to me in Brentwood, but she's not sweet now. "Especially now. Falconsong, let me expel him from the premises."

Capper walks from the fire, standing tall, self-assured, and arrogant as hell. Jane and Madison are crying more than ever. Three witches are still crouching over her, consoling her.

"Jane, are you all right?" I ask.

Capper shoves me to the ground. I'm too surprised to defend myself from him. The warlock grabs my shirt, lifting me up, and then decks me square in the face.

"Cap!" cries Alondra. "Stop it!"

"She told you, dickhead, you're not allowed here!" he says, waving his fist at me. "Now get the fuck out. Or you won't just be hit with my fist."

"Alondra!" I snap, turning on my side, ignoring him. "I saw the ghost. The Ekimmu. I tried to call you. It was the same ghost that was in the house. Winona's ghost. I was in a study group and everything turned dark. I even saw the two little girls again. And then—"

I'm hit hard again. It feels like my face is being rammed against a wall.

"Stop it, Cap!" screams Jane. "Don't touch him!"

Another swing contacts my jaw. I taste blood.

Now, I can hold my own in a fight. I used to box in high school. This guy's really big, but I'm pissed. So I manage to push him away, kick him, then get up and charge him, tackling him like a football player. As he's on the ground, I swing my fist at his face a few times, hard. He wrestles me, spins me, and shoves my face into the dirt with his elbow. Then the asshole pins my arms.

"Cap, stop it!" says Alondra. "Stop it, Lee!"

But I'm strong. I squirm free, spin around, and push him again. As I'm about to swing at his face—

"*Get out, Liam!*" cries Alondra. "*Get out of my yard! Now!*"

I can't believe she's yelling at me.

Capper's face is under my fist. He has a smile on his face, goading me to hit him again.

All the witches circle me with their hoods over their heads. If I weren't used to their cloaks, I think that would be super weird. Well, I suppose it is. Perhaps they're about to cast a spell, or something? But none of it means anything. What really gets me is Alondra's expression. She's angry. Angry at *me*. This fuck jumped me, but Allie's mad at me.

"I saw your ghost again!" I spit at her, rising from the warlock. "I might not be a part of all your shit, but you brought me into this! You have to hear me! I came for your help. I need your help, Allie, whatever the hell you and your witches can do."

"But you can't be here now," Alondra says, shaking her head. She softens a little, but I don't care anymore. "You have to go."

"Come on, fucker." Capper is brushing blood from his lips, goading me to hit him. "We're not done."

"Some other time," I say, wiping more blood from my lip. "Alondra, if you and your witches here have power, you have to help me. I saw that demon again. I—"

"*Exite*," whisper all the witches in unison, surrounding me, "*exite, vade in domum tuam.*" They're all circling me like a flock of ravens. "*Exite, exite, exite vade in donum tuam.*"

"Alondra," I say. But Alondra's turned her back to me and is walking back to the fire.

"Impossible," Alondra mutters, shaking her head, putting her forehead in her hand. "Liam... not now." But she won't turn and look at me.

"*Exite, exite, exite.*"

All the weirdos in their black hoods are looking down at me, as I'm on my knees, chanting the words over and over again.

"Bye-bye," Capper says with an annoying smirk, waving his hand.

I'm thrown to the ground by some invisible force. It reminds me of what happened to Jane in the kitchen that night. But this isn't the middle of the night. And I'm not drunk or drugged. I'm not being pushed by Capper. It seems the air itself threw me to the ground and is dragging me.

"*Exite, exite,*" all the witches echo as if reciting some kind of incantation. "*Exite vade in domum tuam. Exite. Exite.*" The witches keep repeating these words. The words grow louder and louder, reverberating in my head. "*Exite. Exite.*"

I'm sliding along the dirt and mud now. As I'm pulled by nothing across her yard, I take one last glance. They're all creepily standing, facing me, with their heads hidden under their hoods. They don't look human. These dark shadows remind me of the surrounding trees. But two of the witches aren't with them. Jane and Alondra. Jane's still sitting with

Alondra, on white plastic chairs, holding Madison and weeping.

"*Exite. Exite. Exite vade in domum tuam. Exite. Exite.*"

I manage to climb back to my feet. I trip. Stumble. Then I get up and run.

16

MYRTLE BEACH

My friend Bill is sitting in a wicker chair, staring at the beach, watching the scantily clad girls playing by the waves. That's why he chose the patio. Well, it's warm. And that's why we could meet at Myrtle Beach. It's unusually warm this time of year. We're on a wooden deck with the sounds of waves crashing on the shore. The sun and smell of the ocean is a relief. Bill's wearing a preppy button-down and slacks while I'm in a T-shirt and jeans. He managed to slip me a beer. He claimed he was buying a second for himself.

"Will you relax?" he says with a smile, under his shades. "Jesus, your ass is so tight, Lee, I could use it to pull the cap off the next bottle."

I take a swig of my beer over that and run my fingers along my hair. My hair's getting long. I've been too busy with a freak witch cult to trim it.

He points at me, holding his beer. Then he cocks his head and wags the same finger toward a beachgoer.

"Take a look at her. She's probably freezing near the

water. It might be hot, but the water's ice cold, I bet. Priceless. Myrtle Beach."

I lean forward. Two girls in bikinis are running on the waves.

"Don't be so damn obvious," he says with a laugh.

"You're a pervert." I fall back in my chair and lean on my chin. That lasts a split second as my face stings like hell.

"You ready to tell me what happened to your face?" Bill asks. "Please tell me the guy that did that looks worse."

"I got some swings in."

"I've never been in a fight. My face is quite happy for it. But you still have your teeth and a straight nose."

"Yeah."

"Then all's well," he says with his arms out. Then he gestures back at the beach and the pretty girls.

"It was stormy and snowy in Hawthorne last week," I remark, changing the subject randomly. "I never would have thought I'd be outside on a beach."

"Um-hmm," he says, sipping beer. "What's so urgent that you wanted to meet today? I thought you said everything was going great on the phone."

"It's a good school, but weird."

"You should have done better on your SAT. You could have gone somewhere outside of the forest."

"Screw you."

He laughs.

"What about you? How's Duke?"

"There's a lot of history around these parts," he says, pointing to the sea, ignoring my question. "You know the ghost stories around The Grand Stand?" I shake my head. He counts on three fingers. "There's Alice Flagg, Drunken Jack, and The Gray Man. Alice Flagg was a girl who lost the ring of her beloved before she died. The story goes that she still roams these beaches looking for it. The Gray Man story is similar. Only instead of a ring, he's searching for his true love to warn her of storms. That's the guy I'm studying for school. The Gray Man. You remember Hurricane Hugo?"

I shake my head.

"We forget storms, don't we? Well, The Gray Man was there then too. It's said that every time a hurricane erupts, the tall gray man stands just staring out at the water. I'm suggesting that it could just be a discharge of light creating illusions. But I'm also studying the crazier notion that lightning might cause enough energy to rip the fabric of our reality." He raises an eyebrow over his shades, waiting for me to applaud for him or something. Then he points at me with his beer glass. "That's the cool stuff."

"I'm happy for you," I quip sarcastically.

"But today, I'm not working, I'm here for my friend," he says with a wide gesture of his arms, leaning back in his chair, "I got an underaged freshman a beer. What more could you want? So, now tell me—what happened to you? You might want to get that checked. You could have broken your jaw."

"I can move my mouth fine."

"You guys decide on anything?" asks a waitress. She has long blond hair and is wearing a crop top with blue shorts. She's not much older than we are. I quickly push my half-drunk beer closer to him.

"Potato skins," Bill says. "You, Lee?"

She nods then she squints and scrutinizes me. Probably checking out how old I am.

"I'm good."

"Oh, and another beer," Bill adds.

She looks suspiciously at his bottle, which is still three-quarters full. Of course, mine is nearly empty.

"You drink fast," I quip with a grin.

"Well, you need more. So what happened? Attacked by a bear in the woods?"

"There's a lot of weird shit in Hawthorne," I repeat. I love the guy, but how am I going to explain everything? Alondra? Witches? Ghosts?

He's staring at me behind his shades.

I grab my beer bottle. "Hawthorne's cliquey. It's a small college and it's hard to not join a group. If you don't join somewhere, you're a loner."

"I thought there was only one sorority and a couple of fraternities? You referring to clubs or something?"

"Sort of."

"And your girlfriend's in one of them?"

"Sort of. What about you, Bill? How's Heather?"

"We broke up," he says, shaking his head.

"And your students? How's teaching—"

"Forget me. Tell me more about your face."

"My girlfriend's clique had a party. I wasn't invited. But that's not the worst of it. *She* didn't want me there. But that's not even it. She threw me out because it was against her rules. But she still likes me."

"Fuck her. There's other girls. Like the ones down there on the sand."

"You don't understand. It's not her. It's just her group. She still cares for me."

"Tell her to leave the group."

"She's their leader."

He takes a big sigh and nods. "Then why couldn't she let you in?"

"It's not allowed. It's a witch group."

"A witch group?" he asks with a nod. "Hmm. Of course. You're in the freaky woods. Wicca?"

"It's not Wicca. It's weirder."

"So your new girlfriend did this to your face?"

"No." I laugh. "Every coven has one—"

"Male in its group. I know covens. I'm studying the occult at Duke right now." That was the other reason I wanted to meet him. But even though he might be familiar with "Gray Men" and Wiccans, somehow I don't think he's going to fully grasp Alondra's coven.

"So what's wrong?" he asks.

"I need your help."

The waitress brings another beer and the potato skins. Then she turns to me. I don't have time to push the beer to my friend this time.

"Can I see your driver's license?"

"Look at his face," Bill says. "Can you give the guy a break?"

"You guys are going to get me in a lot of trouble."

"I'm joking," Bill says, grabbing my bottle. He winks at her. "It's my birthday. It's all for me."

She hesitates and shakes her head. Then she looks at me. "If I see you drinking again, I'll have to ask you to leave. Okay? That's the rules."

Bill answers by taking my bottle and downing the rest of my beer in front of her. I laugh. She doesn't. When the coast is clear, he pushes me the fresh bottle.

"Go on," he says.

"It's a long story."

I tell him about goths, bonfires, hooded cloaks, Satanism, orgies, sex, incantations, ghosts, possessions, and a gorgeous wicked witch of the west, with emerald eyes, right out of *The Wizard of Oz*. When the story's finished and after I've finished my second beer, I stare at the beach. I turn back. He's speechless.

"You don't believe me?"

"You people in the woods are so weird," he says with this infuriating smirk. I can't help but laugh. "Well, I've known you for a long time, Liam. You're either crazy and hallucinating or you're telling the truth. You're not creative enough to have made this up. I... I believe part of it. Especially the warlock and your eye."

"It's the truth."

I look down at our table. We got so caught up in the story that we barely ate any of the potato skins. I grab one.

I'm feeling good. I've had two beers. I never drink.

Then I look out at the sky. It's red and gold, turning purple. I hesitantly take off my shades and show my ugly face. It's getting dark enough outside to not be ashamed by anyone seeing me.

"We need to get back at Crapper for that," he says, pointing at my face.

"Capper. I hit him pretty hard too."

"His name is Crapper. Did you check your voicemail?"

"No."

"I'm sure she called you after what happened. What are you going to do?"

"I don't know. The fight put things into perspective. For me, Hawthorne *is* Alondra. And Alondra *is* witches. If you met her you'd understand. If I reject her witches, I leave her. If I leave her, I leave Hawthorne. Even before we met, I was miserable and ready to leave the school. That's what's bothering me. That, the ghost, and Hawthorne."

"Well, I'd like to meet her. These sex orgies sound pretty dope."

My expression wipes the smile from his face.

"Sorry," he says, reaching out.

"What can I do about the ghost, Bill? She called it an Ekimmu? Do you know what an Ekimmu is?"

"Are you seriously asking me?"

"Yeah."

"Liam," he says, leaning over with a smirk. "I'm a graduate student *studying* the paranormal and supernatural. I'm here this semester to study phenomena. I don't practice it. I have no idea. You have to go back and ask your girlfriend."

"What's an Ekimmu?"

"Hmm, an Ekimmu is... Sumerian, I think."

"That's what she said."

"Hmm. They were like vampires in ancient times, I think. Demon ghosts. I mean, when you think about it, all ghosts are soul-suckers. They're all using the energy of the living."

"Billy, I saw one tower over me in that girl's room in Alabama. Then, it sounds really stupid, but I swear I saw it again in class. I yelled at it, it disappeared, and it was fucking humiliating."

"Folklore says Ekimmus can latch on to individuals, if I remember correctly. Not like a haunted house, but an actual person. But from your experience in Alabama, maybe you saw what you thought you saw just from all the shock?" That doesn't make me feel any better. "I'm not a ghost hunter, like your weird friends. Maybe ask them. I'm a graduate TA, but..." He lifts a finger. "I'm also your friend. Let me give you a little advice. Join this group. If this girl's in love with you, like you say she is, she'll dump Crapper. Then you can be their high priest and you'll belong just fine."

"I don't want to be a witch." I take a deep breath and drink the last drops of my beer. "Maybe I should take you up on your offer for Duke and go home."

"Well, I might be leaving after Heather. I prefer Myrtle Beach. Or even your orgy forest. I think staying home is what made Heather break up with me in the first place. She wanted to go elsewhere. She was as sick of home as I was."

"I'm lonely as hell in Hawthorne. Alondra's all I got, Bill. If I lose her, I don't have anyone."

"Liam, aside from your face, Hawthorne sounds pretty cool. You're living what I'm studying."

The waitress walks over and hands us the bill.

"Thanks for the beer," I say to Bill.

That gets the waitress all flustered and Bill laughs.

"We're closing the patio," the waitress snaps. "If you want anything else, you can order inside." Then she looks at me. "*He* can order inside."

I'm driving my Camaro over a hundred and twenty-five miles an hour, in the dead of night, back to Hawthorne. I care little for danger and, frankly, I'm enjoying the rush of speed. I figure I'll return to my dorm and sleep two more days until school starts again.

Maybe I've dreamt the whole thing. Maybe I'm fucking crazy, like Bill said. Maybe my girlfriend is crazy too. "*Six, six, six, fucked by a witch?*" What kind of twisted shit is that?

17

———

TACO TUESDAY

I'M TAKING A BREAK FROM MY STUDIES, WATCHING THE cartoon *Ren and Stimpy* on the TV mounted to the wall, thinking of Alondra. I went the whole weekend not talking to her. And, no, Bill was wrong. She didn't leave a voicemail message. She's the omnipotent great goddess Alondra, after all. She probably figured I'd approach her. I won't.

It's Taco Tuesday. I'm alone before a table stacking tortillas, cheddar, lettuce, salsa, and shredded beef on my plate and drinking a Coke from a straw, preparing myself for a feast. Though the plate is stacked, it's all you can eat, so I still might come back for seconds. Hands down, this is the best cuisine the dorm offers students, and the dining hall is packed.

While I'm watching the cat and dog on *Ren and Stimpy* blow each other to bits, I hear my name. I look at a few busy tables behind me but don't see anyone. Then I spot a skinny blonde, in a long multicolored tie-dyed dress, holding the hand of a toddler in a blue dress and bonnet. Everyone's looking at them because no one brings kids into the dining commons. When they reach my table, I finally recognize her. It's Jane. She's holding little Madison's hand.

"Hello," little Maddie says with a wave, cute as hell.

"She's so adorable," says a girl at a nearby table with a chuckle.

"Can we join you?" Jane asks me.

She's not wearing witch makeup. Aside from having brought Maddie, she looks completely normal.

"Sure," I say, getting up. "But you have to pay, right? You're not in the dorm? I can pay for you guys."

"No, no, it doesn't matter, Lee." She asks someone beside us for an extra chair, and she and Maddie sit across from me at my small table. "You're so nice. We just have to talk."

"You want some tacos, Maddie?" I ask her. "It's Taco Tuesday."

"Taco Tuesday," the little tyke repeats, clapping.

"She's got good taste," I say. "So what's up?" I grab some chips from a side dish and place a premade taco on it. I hand it to the toddler as they sit down.

"Your face," Jane says with a frown.

"Don't worry 'bout it. What's going on?"

"My sister died."

"I'm so sorry."

She nods. Then she looks down at Madison.

"That's why you were crying at the Sabbath?" I ask quietly, more to myself.

"My sister's..." She gestures to Madison. "Her mom. It was a car accident. And far worse, my brother-in-law was taken too. That's what we were planning to talk about at the Sabbath before you showed up."

I shake my head. "I'm so sorry to have interrupted."

"No, I'm sorry. Look at what that asshole Cap did to your face." Jane puts her hand to her mouth after saying *asshole* and looks at Madison again. But Maddie is enjoying her taco, paying no attention to our conversation.

"He's such a jerk," she continues. "Madison and I are going away. I'm dropping out of college and taking care of her. I'm going to look for a job and then look after her. I've known her and cared for her ever since she was a baby, anyway. I want the best for her. You know?"

"I'm so sorry, Jane," I say again, reaching out and touching her hand.

Jane's eyes become teary and she nods, fighting back her tears. She looks away. "You're such a nice guy, Lee. I needed to speak with you before I go. I need to talk to you about something."

I nod.

"You said you saw a spirit? An Ekimmu? Ekimmus are demon spirits. They're not like relatives or ghosts that died in the house they haunt. They're much more evil, more like devils. I believe that this Ekimmu was conjured. And now it's haunting you. They don't haunt houses, they haunt people."

"That's why I interrupted you all that night for Alondra's help. Then she tossed me out."

"Oh, Lee, Allie cares about you more than anyone I've ever known. Probably more than herself. But our circle is sacred and is even more important than you. Her witchcraft means everything to her."

"I know."

"I don't think you do. She hurt you and herself."

"I'm not going to pretend that it doesn't hurt, Jane. She hasn't spoken to me since that night."

"She will." And I hate myself for feeling excited about that. I really do. "Anyway, obviously, I'm leaving the coven for good. Alondra and I are best friends, and I haven't told her. Well, I haven't been speaking to her. She'll survive without me, but she'll be devastated. We spend every moment together. But she's strong, like you. It's...tearing me apart. This and Madison."

"What, Momma?" Maddie says, looking up at her.

"Nothing. I love you," Jane says, hugging her and holding her tight. "I just love you so much, Madison. You liking your taco?"

"Um-hmm. Good."

"Try to get it in your mouth, not your dress, dear."

"Alondra can take care of herself, Jane. Don't worry about her. Just worry about you."

"That's just it," she says, and she looks deep in my eyes. It reminds me of the intense way Alondra looks at me sometimes. "She's gone bad, Lee. You don't get what I'm saying. I can't raise Madison in Hawthorne because the coven's gone bad. Normally, I could. But Alondra's turned our circle to left-sided magic. Do you know what that is?"

I nod.

"Evil," she says with a nod. "Satanic. You saw it that night when those girls grabbed you on Hilltop Bluff. Capper's using left-sided magic to empower us. Satanism. An upside-down pentagram. You see, people are dying because Alondra's digging too deep. She's causing the evil she's hunting. She's becoming evil."

"I recall Kenosha saying something similar."

"Allie's been obsessed with evil in the occult ever since she was a child. She wants to know how her parents died. She's convinced they died of witchcraft. And now..." Jane looks at Madison and hesitates. Maddie's face is full of meat and cheese. Jane wipes her face with a napkin. "Well."

"I get it. Why do you think your sister—" I don't finish my sentence because now I'm looking at Madison too.

"There were red pentagrams painted inside the car, Lee. Alondra's uncle told her, when she was a teenager, those same red pentagrams were splashed all over her parent's clothes after they were shot. At first, her uncle was trying to scare her off from the occult by telling her—ironically, that only made her more determined than ever to experiment with me in high school. They caught the guy who fired the rifle. The guy insisted it was an accident. Not the pentagrams, but the killing. Well, that nut's in jail. So it wasn't him who did this to my sister. But those same symbols were painted in her car. Nut or not, he was a satanist. And I think satanists are coming out and attacking us now because of what Alondra's digging up. Or perhaps the symbols are simply appearing as a curse for all the sins we've done?"

I furrow my brow. If I had heard this a year ago, I probably would have jumped up and run out of the dining hall. But this is the world I live in now.

"Lee. I... I..." She struggles with tears. "I hate her. God, I love Allie so much, but I hate her, Liam. Do you understand?"

Yes. I do.

"She's provoking this. She's looking into things instead of leaving them alone. She's drawing it up from the ground. She's making this darkness manifest into our world. If she had just laid off, this wouldn't have happened. And, god, Liam, it wouldn't have happened to Madison!"

And that's it. Jane falls apart. I grab the nearest napkin and hand it to her.

Madison stops eating. "What's wrong, Momma?"

"I'm not your momma," she snaps between tears. "Christ, I'm not your momma!" But Jane hugs the little girl tight.

I don't know what to say. People from other tables are staring at us. Worse, they are giving me an accusatory look, as if I made her cry.

"I've done this enough," Jane finally says, throwing her napkin down. "I'm not here to cry. This demon that's haunting you is Alondra's fault. Whatever witch is attacking her, they know you're getting involved with her, and by attacking you, they get to her. That's why Alondra hasn't called you. After what happened to me, she's scared something will happen to you. But I had to tell you why. You two are close. You fit one another, Lee, but...I'm sorry, you have to stay away from her. She's right to keep you away. The evil, the satanism, it's going to consume you if you don't stay away. It's who she is now. It's her."

Jane takes a deep breath and shakes her head.

So many are staring at us. I'm about ready to jump up and shout at everyone to mind their business. Then it dawns on me. My bruised face and the child sitting at the table. They're probably thinking about domestic violence or something.

"I'm sorry," Jane says, looking around, seemingly noticing too.

"You okay, Momma?" Madison asks Jane. It is so adorable, it actually makes me chuckle. Jane nods.

I make another taco for her.

"You're so sweet, Lee," Jane says, dabbing her eyes with the napkin again.

After I hand Madison the taco, I ask, "Who is after Alondra? What coven?"

"An Abaddon coven."

"Kenosha mentioned this. Where is this Abaddon coven?"

"It's just a name. It's ancient Hebrew for "destruction." It's used by witches who have forsaken this world, seeking only pleasure. They have completely given themselves to it. It's not just ritual or left-sided rites, it means complete worship of evil—the devil, if you're Christian. Loving nature and the world can be good. There are good witches and there are good forces. But if they learn to seek pleasure at the cost of other people's pain, they become evil. I don't think Alondra has gone that far herself. *Yet.* Maybe Cap has. But it doesn't matter. She's drawn power from her devil worshipping, and that, itself, is enough to come back and harm us."

"Where is this evil coven?"

"I don't know. That's what Alondra's spent her whole life searching for. But I'll tell you this, that demon you saw haunting Winona was summoned by a witch. It is not just a ghost. We've talked about that at our Sabbath too. Even after you left, Alondra spoke of what could be done to help you. I told you, she only cares about you and the craft."

Again, I feel good after that. Then I curse myself for being stupid.

"That other witch was with you in Alabama, right?" Jane asks. "You mentioned her. The high priestess of the Crescent coven? Kenosha?"

"You don't think Kenosha did this to me, do you? Have you met her? She doesn't have a bad bone in her body. She's as nice as you."

"Evil disguises itself well," Jane says with a shrug. "Allie's suspicious of Kenosha. Alondra found old Escoba's grimoire a couple years ago. We think Kenosha's always resented her use of her coven's grimoire. Kenosha holds a great deal of power, whether it be right or left magic. I've also thought of Capper." She shakes her head almost violently. "I doubt it. He hates you, but the idiot doesn't know you all that well, and he isn't even that powerful. It doesn't matter. That's not why I'm here. Leave Alondra. It's all because of her. She'll bring the Abaddon witch to your doorstep if you continue to be with her. She'll hurt you. I told you, she hasn't called you because she's afraid she will. She will. I'm leaving because I know she'll hurt me and Madison."

I just nod.

But then my body feels heavy. My eyes wander to *Ren and Stimpy*, a cartoon that I love, on the TV monitor hanging on the wall. It seems particularly stupid. It's always stupid, but with my sudden depression, it's stupid in a bad way. It dawns on me that this sudden weight is the familiar finale that I've experienced many times at the end of a crush. It makes me realize how much I was into Alondra, how much I don't want to lose her.

"I'm sorry, Lee. Please do what Madison and I are doing. Get out. Go. Now. Alondra can't control her magic anymore. If it doesn't get rid of her, it'll get rid of everyone around her."

"She's good—"

"I know she's good! Damn it!" Jane quickly turns to Madison. Indeed, the girl jumped over the outburst. Jane just flashes a fake smile at the little girl. Then she leans her head in her hand. "I blame her for Madison. Allie won't stop. My god, even if you're gone, she'll keep this up. She didn't start all bad. But now the coven's upside down. She will do everything, even if it destroys her, to find this Abaddon witch. But she'll never admit to the evil herself."

"I have to try to help her then."

"You'll be taken too." And that really pisses her off. She seems angry at me. She jumps up. "I have to go. Sorry. But I warned you."

She gets up, but I reach for her. "Jane, how do I get rid of this demon? If I can't talk to Allie, who can I turn to? Who else can rid me of the possession?"

Jane hesitates. It's like she never thought of that. Madison looks over and furrows her brow at Jane. "I don't know. I'm...so sorry. But I don't want to be a witch anymore. I can't help you... Goodbye."

I get up, walk around the table, and surprise her with a hug. "If there's anything I can do for you, let me know, Jane."

"You're...my god, Liam," she says in my arms squeezing tight. "She's so lucky to have found you."

"Take care of yourself."

"No. *You* take care of yourself."

I kneel and give little Madison a hug.

"Bye, bye," Maddie says with a grin.

18

———

WHITECHAPEL

I'm studying in my dorm room for a final tomorrow. It's my criminology exam. And that reminds me of Alondra. Well, I suppose every little thing reminds me of Alondra lately. It's Thursday and it's been a week since I've spoken to her. I remember Jane's warning, but I'm finding it harder and harder to accept. I'm on the verge of driving to her house tonight. Because, like I've already told you, I'm an idiot.

It's a bit creepy going over Jeffrey Dahmer and his eating habits with all the darkness outside. It's foggy and super dark tonight. My dorm room has been empty since my roommate left at the beginning of the year, and it's times like these that I wish he was back, or that someone was in the room. Anyway, I'm reviewing how Dahmer sexually molested his victims and then ate their flesh.

I jump at a knock. I crack open the door.

Alondra.

She's standing there wearing her red "Hawthorne" sweater and blue jeans without any goth makeup. She even has on red lipstick. That all bothers me. It's manipulative. I don't like how she wears witch makeup or not based on her predicament.

She smiles sweetly. That feels manipulative too. "Hi," she says with a wave.

"I haven't heard from you since your house."

"Your face," she says, wrinkling her brow and reaching to touch it. I step back. "Oh, Liam. Does it hurt?"

"I'm fine. You could have called?"

"You didn't call either."

Touché.

"I've never been in your dorm at night," she says, trying to peek over my shoulder. "Makes me curious."

"Why are you here?"

"I've never been in your dorm at night," she repeats with a shrug.

"Alondra...it's just—"

"You need a study partner," she says, wagging her finger at me. She smiles. "Test's tomorrow."

Her green eyes stare into mine. She doesn't need to say another word. If I wasn't angry, I'd grab her, pull her inside, lock my lips on hers, and be uncontrollably lost in making out with her—I'm so attracted to her. But I'm still angry.

"Allie—"

"Allie," she says bitterly with a sad nod. "I like it so much when you call me that. Please call me Allie, Liam." *Because only her best friend and I call her Allie. And Jane's left her.*

"Come in," I say.

She walks in, closes the door behind us, and checks out my small room. Of course, it's a pig sty. I quickly move shirts and pants from the chair and bottom bunk.

She plops down on the bottom bunk. Then she gazes out the dark window.

"There's going to be a building out there in a few years," she says. "Right now, there's just an empty lot, if you peer through all tonight's fog. I know because sometimes I can tell the future. Did you know that?"

"Nothing surprises me about you anymore, Allie," I say, rummaging through my desk. I grab my textbook. "But it's not hard to imagine a building there with an empty lot."

"I see this dorm has significance for something." And she's staring outside. "Something that will happen to someone else who will one day hold my book *Broomstick*."

"What's *Broomstick*?"

"My book," she says, turning back with her lovely emerald gems. "Don't you remember? The one at Winona's."

I hand her my textbook. Our class textbook, not her freaky witch book. Then she sits on the bottom bunk, and I sit down on my wooden desk chair across from her.

"Thanks," she says, grabbing the book. "I see lots of highlighting. Good boy. What serial killer would you like to talk about?"

"How about Alondra Billington?"

It's meant as a joke, but it's not received well. She loses all her joy and playfulness. Then I remember Jane. She quickly turns from me. I didn't mean to hurt her that much.

"Sorry."

"I can't believe Capper hit you in the face. I didn't want you there, but he was a total jerk. He's heard an earful from me over that, believe me. I'm probably going to cast him out of our coven."

"It doesn't hurt that much anymore."

"He has quite a shiner too," she says, turning back. Her eyes are teary. "I didn't know you were such a slugger."

"I used to box in high school."

"Hmm." She thumbs through my textbook. "Well, I'm not a serial killer, Liam."

"I know."

"Yeah. But Jane's not so sure."

"She came by and told me she was leaving in the dining commons. She warned me about you. She said I should stay away from you."

"She's probably right. You should. But we've had this discussion before. You like fast cars."

"Why are you here?"

She squints at me as if I'm stupid. Then she gives me her infamous sweet smile. I'm hating that smile right now. "Lee, the only way I'd never see you again is if I became a serial killer and killed you."

"That doesn't make me feel any better."

"That's not all," she says with a laugh. "Even though we cast you out of our meeting, you spoke of a haunting. A demon haunting you is very serious. If a ghost followed you after our exorcism, it could be that the spirit now resides in you. I told you you're forbidden to attend our sabbaths, but that doesn't mean I don't want to get rid of what's trying to harm you. So I'm here to ask you to do something you probably don't want to do."

"What's new?"

"Is that really fair?" she asks, serious again.

I shake my head.

"I'm inviting you to our Sabbath this week."

"Are you serious, Allie!" I surprise myself with my tone. "Why? This is so you. This is just like Kenosha and Winona's room. You guys forbid, forbid, and forbid, I get into a brawl with your *high priest*, then you tell me to come back the week after and join. I don't get you guys."

"I'm not asking you to join. I don't know any other way to get rid of this demon. I've called Kenosha to bring another expert to help you at our Sabbath. She is traveling very far. If you have an Ekimmu haunting you, like Winona—and I believe you do if you say you do—then you're in big trouble. They stick, Lee. It's gonna take a lot of magic to get it out."

I stare at her. She seems to think that's funny and chuckles. Then she shrugs and flips through my textbook again.

"Jane doesn't want to talk to me anymore," she says with a shrug. "Did she tell you that? That hurts a lot. It's not proven that witchcraft killed Maddie's parents. Jane believes it did. She claims that when I used her to rid us of the poltergeist with left-sided magic, she and her family were cursed as reciprocation for using the backward pentacle. Maybe. But that hardly means it's my fault. We expelled the poltergeist and helped Maybelle and Alice, if you remember. Wasn't that good? Well..." She takes a deep breath, thumbing through more pages. "I don't totally blame her for being mad. But I love Jane. What happened to her sister is so horrible. But I don't accept her blame. I don't. That's not fair." She seems to finally find the page she was looking for. "Has that demon haunted you since the night you came to our Sabbath?"

"No."

"Good. Many ghosts appear due to stress. It's like the deer we saw when we fucked in the motel room. Stress makes for powerful magic."

She smiles slyly. I can feel the attraction. And I'm reminded what Jane said about her. Yes, exactly like Jane, I love and hate her at the same time.

She runs her long fingernail, colored witchy black, along a page and asks, "Tell me who the Whitechapel Murderer is? You don't have much highlighting here. I wonder if you read this chapter."

I fold my arms, lean back in my chair, and look at her blankly.

"I'll give you a hint, handsome, red-haired Irish boy," she says. "Bloody Sunday, 1887."

I shrug.

"God, I'm glad I came." She takes a deep breath, closes

the book, and leans forward. "You really don't know? Bloody Sunday was the famous Irish revolt in London in 1887. This is not to be confused with the U2 song "Sunday Bloody Sunday"—which you probably love, since we have the same taste in music—about the British soldiers who opened fire on the Irish in 1972. In Whitechapel, in 1888, this serial killer I'm alluding to went on a rampage. A very famous one. He preferred prostitutes, which were all over this seedy district. Authorities thought he suffered from satyriasis. There's a psychology term for your major. Satyriasis is…" She winks. "A sudden uncontrollable sex urge. Like a witch's wandering. In women, they used to call it nymphomania. You've heard that word, right?"

"Only *this* killer murdered his women after sex," I say.

"I told you, I'm not a serial killer, Liam," she says, shaking her head and looking back at our book. "I'm not a killer at all. I'm a witch."

"Jack the Ripper," I answer.

"You got it! You did read it."

"The century's a giveaway. I didn't remember the dates and all your other facts. How do you remember all those things, Allie?"

"I don't know. I've always been good with dates. Jack the Ripper killed between 1888 and 1891. Dr. Kriegel loves dates. And he'll grade you an A if you throw them around in your essay. Remember that this silly psycho killer course is really a way to study history, so pour on the extra stuff in your essay. Did the police ever catch Jack?"

I shake my head. She nods.

She's back to looking through our textbook. "Okay… and…" She plops her finger near the beginning of the text-book. "Here. Let's go forward to more current stuff. Tell me the—"

But I snatch the book from her hands.

"Hey!"

"My turn." But then I don't even look at the book. I look into her eyes with the book sitting on my lap. For a moment, I get lost in those damned eyes again. She smiles. "Tell me the name of the Greek who snatched weary travelers and forced them to fit into his beds by either stretching them on a rack or cutting their limbs."

She smiles but then she rolls her eyes as if it's too easy. "Procrus-something-or-other."

"You don't know the name?"

"We won't need to know exact names for the test. We can either omit them on the essay or guess based on the the *procrus* part in the multiple choice section."

"Procrustes."

"How do you remember the name?"

"I like Greek mythology."

"I don't think we're gonna be going that far back in history tomorrow." She shrugs and snatches the textbook back. "But I can see you've been a good boy and read the whole textbook. You wanna go far back, huh? Okay."

She's back to flipping pages, and I'm enjoying watching her pale fingers move through each page and her furrowing her brow and smiling to herself. She's thinking, and I enjoy thinking about how she's thinking about stuff. I tell you, I'm hooked. So? Sue me.

"Ah, this one. Who is the serial killer in history with the most kills? There's something not to be proud of."

I can't recall. I'm too busy enjoying watching her. She looks right into my eyes again and raises an eyebrow, cute as hell. Then she throws her long dark hair back.

I shrug my shoulders.

She deflates hers. "Oh, come on."

"I think it was in the fifteenth century or something?

Some freak they tortured for a really long time because he kept a log of his kills."

"Who? And don't joke with *Alondra Billington* again. This was a man. You might have noticed they were sexist even with the list of serial killers in history."

"I don't know."

"Think of a backward cross. *Christ*-man. Cause you'll never get the name." She looks at the book and reads: "Christman Genipperteinga. The book says he lived in Germany in the sixteenth century and logged nine hundred and sixty-four kills. The freak was disappointed that he didn't hit a thousand."

"I thought you said we don't need to memorize all the names."

"Yeah, but don't you love saying that name: *Genipperteinga*?" And she laughs real hard and touches my hand. "You won't forget it now."

"Next," she says, raising a finger and flipping through more pages.

As she's flipping, her fingers slow and she loses her mirth. She seems to get very serious. She puts the book on her lap for a moment and stares down at it.

"Do you mind if I stay here for the night? I'm... having a hard time."

I think if she was a different sort of girl, she'd cry. I come over and sit by her on the bed. She leans on my shoulder.

"I don't care what Jane says," she says quietly, "I have to be with you." She wipes her eyes. She snuggles deeper into my side. "I'm so sorry," she says quietly. "God, I'm so sorry I hurt you. You don't even know how much. I'd rather Cap have hit me. You come to our Sabbath again like that and, whatever the rules, you're welcome. I don't care anymore. Okay?"

"I'm sorry too."

She moves from my arm and peers deeply in my eyes. Her eyes are moist. A tear runs down from those green gems. "Our first fight," she says with a sad smile. She very gently touches the side of my face, which is still bruised, and frowns again.

I put my arms around her and embrace her more tightly.

"I think I'm falling in love with you, Lee," she says quietly. "I really am."

19

CREEPERS

I CAN'T SLEEP. IT'S NOT ALONDRA BREATHING OVER ME ON THE top bunk keeping me up. That's loud, but soothing. It's that I haven't slept since Winona and her possession. The image of that lanky creep keeps popping up in my mind. And this isn't like some scene from a scary movie. It was real.

I'm tossing and turning. I open my eyes and stare at the bunk above. The moonlight is shining over my face through the closed curtain. And, even though it's like three in the morning, I hear people occasionally walking down the hallway outside my room. Oh, and my face still stings. The pain doesn't help me sleep either.

"Lee," Alondra whispers, "are you sleeping?"

She's up now too. "No. I thought you were."

I hear her moving over the sheets with the creaking of the upper planks. Then I see her shadow fall by my side. She's wearing one of my T-shirts and her panties. It's warm enough inside. I'm just in underwear. Which is a bit shameful after she surprises me by lifting my sheets and gently climbing under the covers with me.

"What are you doing?" I whisper.

She smells nice. It's always some natural scent. Tonight, it's festive, like pumpkin and cinnamon. I feel her run her fingers along my hair and kiss the back of my head. It's a habit of hers. She loves my hair.

She puts an arm around me and runs her fingers along my arm.

"Can't sleep. I thought you could use some company. Did I wake you?"

"No. Worried about the final?"

"Are you kidding?" she says with a snicker. "I could teach the class."

"That's true."

"You?"

"No. We went over everything."

I lie on the pillow and she nuzzles her head against mine.

"You're warm," she says. "Why aren't you sleeping?"

"I haven't slept well since Alabama. I can't stop thinking of the demon."

"I should never have taken you there. But you haven't seen it since that class, you told me?"

"No, but his image is burned into my head."

"Try to forget it. We can try to fall asleep together."

So I start drifting off thinking that I actually might sleep in her arms. I'm okay with that. And, I suppose, being in my girlfriend's arms works 'cause I find myself getting drowsier.

I jerk awake. Alondra, who's still holding me, is shaking. She's whimpering.

"What's the matter?" I ask.

"I'm sorry," she says in a broken voice. "God, Lee, I want out of my coven. That day you ran from my house, I didn't blame you. I wanted to run away with you. Let me run away to Atlanta with you. Jane's right. Let's run away together and leave Hawthorne forever."

I turn and she digs her head into my chest and cries some more.

"It's okay," I whisper as she shakes.

"Hold me. Please." And, this time, she turns so her back is to me. There's not a whole lot of room in the bed.

My fingers glide over her back. I massage her skin.

"That's nice."

She takes my hand and brings it under her shirt, my shirt, touching her chest. I feel lace.

"It's the bra in the store," she says with a giggle. "Remember?" She wipes her eyes. Then runs my hand under the bra and over the curves of her naked breast and nipple. "Even better."

I feel very aroused. I'm hard. She seems to notice and pushes her butt against my erection.

"I didn't sleep in the same bed to be naughty. Honest." She turns and our lips touch, then our tongues. "But maybe I should have," she adds with a giggle.

I touch her other breast, near the sheet but, before I know it, she takes my hand and moves it between her legs. I've never touched a woman between her legs before. She guides my finger inside her. She moans.

"Oh, Lee," she says, breathless. "Kiss me."

She is moving my finger gently in and out of her. I readjust, feeling harder. Then she lets go, but I don't stop stroking her. Meanwhile, she probes my leg until her hand lands on my erection. She moves her hand up and down over my underwear, kissing me hard on the lips again. The kiss reminds me of her hard, passionate kissing during her wandering in the motel. Then she reaches inside my underwear and touches my bare cock.

"Maybe," she says between kisses. "Maybe we *should* be naughty tonight. Eh, tiger?"

She yanks down her panties under the sheets and

throws them off the bed. Then she moves on top of me, mounting me. She reaches back and lifts her shirt over her head, revealing the lace bra. Then she unlatches the bra from behind. Her pale breasts shine in the moonlight and a streetlight shining through the partially open drapes. I can just make out her face, her gentle smile. She rocks slowly back and forth over my underwear. I groan. She opens her eyes wider over that.

She leans down and kisses my lips tenderly again. As she presses her groin over mine, we make out some more and I can hear the sound of our wet lips. She whispers in my ear, "I said *fuck* earlier because I adore watching you get aroused, Liam. You blush. I want to *fuck* that. I want to *fuck* that right now."

She yanks my underwear off under the sheets and tosses it from the bed, like she did with hers. Then she pulls the sheets off us and straddles me again with her breasts close to my face. She leans even closer because her head is nearly touching the bunk above. Then she grinds against me again, moving faster and moaning.

She repositions. I'm surprised to see that just a slight change in position helps her manage to work my cock inside her.

My heart races, but not only from arousal now, from fear. I didn't have time to get a condom. Am I too late? She was so fast. Being neurotic, I start thinking of STDs. I think of Rachel and Capper and all the other initiates in ceremonies she's possibly made love to. I think of Jane's warning again, and wonder if this is how she's going to hurt me. She's going to get me sick with a sexually transmitted disease from unprotected sex. It makes me want to get her off me. But she's moving faster. Harder. And it feels so good.

"I need to get a condom," I say, breathless.

"I'm clean, Liam," she says, shaking her head.

"We should stop," I push her to the side, but she's still pushing me inside her. "We should stop. Let me get one."

"Lee, I'm clean." She lies over me again and sucks my lips. She's breathing heavily over my face. I smell her breath. It's spearmint. It mixes delightfully with her pumpkin and cinnamon perfume. "I've been tested. Don't worry, babe."

"But what about protection? Are you on the pill?"

She quickly shakes her head and that makes me feel worse.

"But ..." She stretches back, presenting her breasts in full view. Then, as she grinds some more, she runs my hand along her curves. "I've been thinking we should make a baby." She brings up my hand and kisses it. "I want your child. That...that...way I can have an angel just like you."

"Alondra, no. I need—"

"Oh, Lee," she says, breathless. "Relax. Fuck me. Fuck me, now. Don't stop. You feel so good. Please."

"Were you joking about protection?"

I see a hint of a grin in the shadows, but I'm not sure. Then she shakes her head again.

"Alondra, just get off."

"*Fuck!*" She cries out in pleasure, her whole body shaking over me. And she doesn't stop shaking. Her breasts shake over me too as she presses hard into me.

Then she lies on top of me completely still, as if resting for a moment.

But she's not done. She's at it again down below, lifting her hips up and down slowly. Her arms are wrapped around my back while she moans beside my ear. Then she speeds up, breathing heavier, thrusting faster and faster, again and again, up and down my cock, while clutching me tightly. I hear her pelvis smacking into mine now. "Yes. Oh, fuck! Yes. Yes! Oh, yes, fuck me, Lee!" She's crying out so loud I'm guessing the whole dormitory can hear her. "Take me! *Fuck me!*"

She quakes again in my arms. *"Fuck!"* Then she pushes off of my chest and leans back displaying her tits in full view. Her whole body shakes again. *"Yes! Fuck!"*

That does it. I lose control and orgasm inside her.

There's complete silence. She's lying on top of me, and I only hear her heavy breathing.

She runs her tongue over my cheek with a giggle.

I'm nervous. I came inside her.

"What's the matter?" she whispers in my ear.

"Nothing."

"Shh," she says, stroking my face. "Everything will be fine. You always worry too much. Just rest, babe."

My eyes jerk open at the sound of a baby crying. It's like I fell asleep again. Did I drift off to sleep and she went back on the top bunk? But how do I hear a baby crying in the room?

"Look, Lee," Alondra says. "Ahhh, look what we made."

I scoot, naked, off the bed and stand up, climbing up to look over the top bunk. Alondra is shining a small flashlight over a crying baby lying on her stomach.

"Look, Lee. She's not human."

Alondra shines the flashlight over a faceless baby. There are no eyes or mouth. And blood is dripping down its body over Alondra's naked breasts and stomach. It's squirming like a worm. "She's not human, Liam, but it's okay with you, right? Because she's ours. She's all ours. And I love my two little angels."

I turn away in disgust.

Standing in the dark shadows of my dorm room, near

the window, is a very tall lanky spirit lit by the moonlight. He's nearly touching the ceiling. His eyes shine white, but he's faceless. He emits the loudest shriek I've ever heard.

~

I jump in bed. I'm sweating. My body's shaking.

"What's the matter?" asks Alondra sluggishly in the upper bunk.

"Just a dream."

She yawns and slides from the top bunk. That scares me because she's wearing the same T-shirt and panties as she was in my dream.

"I just had a nightmare."

"I can't sleep well either," Alondra says with a yawn. She kneels by the bed and reaches out to me.

"Don't say that," I say nervously, pushing her away. "You said that in my dream."

"I was in your dream?" she asks, surprised, moving away from me. "That's weird."

"What do you mean?"

She lifts the cover to join me—just like in my dream—but I quickly put my hand up, stopping her. I'm not only freaked by the bad dream, but I had a wet dream and my underwear's wet.

"What's wrong?"

I push her aside and jump out of bed. Then I open a drawer and rummage in the dark for a fresh pair of underwear.

"What's wrong?" she asks again, sounding amused.

"Turn around. I have to change."

"Why? Liam, it's three in the morning and pitch dark. I can barely even see you."

"Just turn around and don't look, okay?"

I rummage through my dresser in the dark looking for a fresh pair of underwear. Then I jump back in bed and pull the covers over my body, feeling completely humiliated.

"What's going on?" she asks with a laugh.

"I had a nightmare."

She sits down next to me on the bed and strokes my hair. "Tell me."

She touches the sheet and moves her hand under it, brushing over my bare chest and abs. I throw her hand out.

"What's wrong, Liam?" she asks, again, with a laugh. "You're acting like I have a disease."

Yeah.

I tell her my dream. It's really hard to do. I'm embarrassed as hell, but she listens attentively to the whole thing in the dark silence. Then, without a response, it seems quieter. I don't hear anyone outside my door. It's probably too early in the morning now.

After a while, she says, "You have to join our Sabbath tomorrow."

"Why?"

"The demon is inside you. We need to perform another exorcism. This time with the coven. This isn't normal."

"No, it wasn't normal. It was just a dream."

"No, you had a succubus attack you. I can enter dreams. I'm a witch. I'm in the same room as you and I wasn't in that one."

"That's crazy."

"You saw the demon. You heard the banshee call. In the same room, there's no way I wouldn't have entered your mind and not gotten involved in all that baby nonsense if you weren't possessed. Do you think I want a baby?" She laughs. I don't laugh with her. "Uh, no, Lee. I love you and all, but no. This was your demon haunting you in the form of a succubus."

"So, I wasn't having sex with you, but with—"

"A succubus."

"I don't want to talk about this anymore, Alondra. It's really weird."

"I get it. Goodnight then." She climbs back up to the upper bunk. "Get some sleep." She yawns. "You have a high priestess watching over you. If weird stuff starts happening again, call my name. Say something in your dream like "I invoke Alondra Billington." Then I will come down and kick some ghost ass."

"You're making fun of me."

"Sorry, I'm trying to lighten your mood. It's also the witching hour. Everything feels weird now. Goodnight, Liam." She adjusts in bed in the upper bunk and I hear the planks move. Then she yawns. "Come to our Sabbath tomorrow. It'll be great comeuppance for Capper. He'll hate it that you're there. We need to discuss all this with the group."

"I'm not going to discuss my sex dream with the group!"

Alondra laughs really hard. She can't stop. "We don't have to talk about that."

"Goodnight, Alondra. Let's worry about our final exam first."

There's silence again in the darkness. Then, I don't know how much later, she says, "Lee, I'd never hurt you."

"You didn't want to hurt me in the dream, either," I say, staring up at the planks of the upper bed in the darkness.

"I did something against your will."

"Alondra, your coven partakes in ceremonial sex. You might want to argue it's consent and not rape, but whatever the lie, it's not love. And it's with a backwards pentagram. Isn't that hurting people?"

"It's complicated."
More silence. I'm almost drifting off…
"I care about you, Lee. You're my angel."
I cringe. She said that word in my nightmare.

20

THE MIRROR

I'm sitting on a stool in Alondra's master bathroom and, like the rest of the house, her bathroom is simply amazing. In front of me is a large mirror with these fancy gold columns around it and a marble sink. Even the faucets are gold, hooking over like huge swan necks into a gold basin. There's another large gilded vanity mirror to my side. Even the stool I'm on is bordered in gold. It's all brass, for sure, but elegant as hell.

Alondra is standing over me. She's already decked out in her black cloak and goth makeup. Now it's my turn.

She's been giggling while getting ready for the past hour. I really don't care. Honestly, my fears are far greater over the prospect of summoning ghosts and demons than looking like a clown. But after acing our psycho killer final together, she reminded me about the Sabbath. Then, somehow, she convinced me that I needed to be prepared.

"Take your baseball cap off," she says.

"Will you stop laughing?"

"Sorry." She leans over and kisses me on the cheek. "You're really going to let me do this?"

"If you think it'll help get me accepted in your clique, then yes. If you're planning on doing it for your friends to make fun of me, then no."

"You're gonna look hot," she says. But I can tell she's holding back from bursting into laughter again.

"Okay, first blush," she says. She takes out a big thick brush and starts dabbing my cheeks.

"What's this for?" I pull back.

"We need to pale your cheeks."

"Aren't I pale enough?"

She ignores me and starts brushing my skin with white stuff. "Be still, Liam. You move around and this is going to take longer." I turn and she pulls my chin closer. "And keep straight." She kisses my lips.

"Cut it out."

Then she runs the whitening gently over the bruises I still have from last week. "I can't wait for Cap to see you. Just turn, not that way, look straight into the mirror."

"There," she says staring at my face quite earnestly. "Better."

Then she takes out another brush and works on my eyebrows. Next it's eyeshadow. She confuses me a little when she brings in a little bit of red. I thought it'd all be black. Well, black is brushed over that.

"I'm nervous."

"Because you're adorable," she says, brushing the colors in.

"I feel ridiculous. But I'm not talking about that. I'm talking about tonight. You want to tell me what to expect?"

She turns very serious. She sifts through the cabinets for something more to add. She carries it over and lays it on the counter before us. It's a couple of eyelashes.

"I don't know," she says. "All I know is we have to get rid of what's haunting you. I have two experts coming."

"Other than dreams, I haven't seen it since last week."

"It's there." She takes a sponge over my cheek. "Now we're gonna manifest it ourselves by me inviting you to our coven tonight. That'll mean that the spirit will have to attack my entire coven when it attacks you."

She's putting something on the fake eyelash.

"What's that?"

"Adhesive. Eyelash glue. Now be still, Lee."

"Why do you have to add eyelashes?"

"You wanted to look goth. Ah-ight?"

"No, *you* wanted me to look goth. I already do. My eyelashes are fine as they are."

"Your lashes are wonderful. But you don't look goth enough. Let me deal with Capper tonight. Keep your fiery temper to yourself. Let me fight him. He's a real idiot. A lamb, actually, if you get to know him. But he struts his feathers. If you strut back, the two of you are just going to end up in another cockfight. Let me take care of him. In our coven, he's subservient to me. Don't fall in—" She's trying to place the eyelashes over mine. She turns my chin again. "Keep still, Liam. You want me to get the glue inside your eyes?"

"May I remind you that I was sucker punched. I didn't start that fight."

She nods. After she puts on the other eyelash, she turns my head to the side then straight to the mirror again. Then she kisses my cheek again with a giggle.

She rustles through another cabinet and takes out a hairbrush.

"I know what that is."

She smiles and nods. Then she makes me feel like she's a hairdresser, only I usually don't look like a vampire when I'm looking in the mirror. Honestly, I don't like what I see. In my high school back home, I would have gotten beaten up looking like this. But somehow in Hawthorne, it's vogue.

She starts brushing my hair.

"I can do this part."

"I know. But I like doing it."

I snatch the brush and roll my eyes. She leans down and kisses my lips with a laugh. "Ooh, I like kissing my warlock."

"Stop it," I say, between kisses.

"There's one last important part," she says, raising a finger.

Lipstick. She leans over holding her black lipstick near my lips. I stop her just in time with my palm. I shake my head. Lipstick is not happening. She shrugs. Then she moves my head around again, staring at her work in the large mirror.

"You look scary," she says with a laugh. "Menacing. But cute as hell."

21

———

ABADDON

"TONIGHT WE CELEBRATE YULE." ALONDRA SPEAKS LOUDLY TO the whole group in a circle. "The sacred night of darkness."

I'm trying not to shiver but it's cold. I crunched over ice on the grass as we walked into Alondra's backyard. The big bonfire at the center of the field helps warm me a little as we sit on plastic chairs, but I still shake. Even Alondra seems to be fighting to keep her teeth from chattering.

Allie's sitting to my immediate right. Her friend Rachel is to my left—that's the one who was naked on the *x*, being fucked by Capper that night on Hilltop Bluff. I try not to think about that. I feel ridiculous in makeup. But, not surprisingly, her friends barely notice. The black cloak with a hood doesn't help me feel better either. After I'd complained throughout dinner, Alondra finally suggested I pretend like I'm a play actor. That worked until I saw Capper's expression.

"The turning of the wheel moves us from darkest night to greatest light," Alondra says with a smile. "*Lux alba.* Tonight, friends, we have a special guest, a dear friend of mine, to celebrate with us. Meet Liam." Alondra gestures to me. "Please stand, Liam. As your high priestess, I ask that we all welcome you to my coven."

Everyone gets up. It startles me that everybody was so solemn, staring at the ground. Now they approach me all smiley.

"Rachel," says the blond girl to my left, clasping my hand. Well, I know her.

"Holly," says an Asian girl with a wave. Her head is shaven and she wears a nose ring and multiple earrings. She's the one who led the group in throwing me out of Alondra's yard. But she's smiling too now.

"Beth," says a dark-skinned witch, the youngest in the group. She's one of the two drugged witches who attacked me on Hilltop Bluff. She hugs me. "Yatu, Liam. Welcome to the circle."

"Catherine," says a pale girl with a shaved head. "May you never thirst."

The whole circle introduces themselves, and I try to remember each name. Many I met at the house of the poltergeist, but I'm terrible at names. The last is the one and only Capper.

"Lucifer," he says, with a stupid smirk, in his Australian accent. He squeezes my hand mercilessly tight. "Nice face. Pleasure to serve you for dinner tonight."

"Crapper," I reply with a nod.

Alondra quickly turns to me. *Crapper* narrows his eyes but then returns to his seat. We all do.

"Welcome, Liam," Alondra says, regaining her smile. "The Hawthorne coven welcomes you. Blessings come from Hecate. Glory be Astraeus. Let not clouds block Selene. And if it be, let the rays of light come from within. Atman. *Lux alba.*"

"*Lux tenebris,*" says Capper, seemingly forgetting my

insult. He bows his head as if in prayer, but afterward, he resumes glaring at me across the fire.

"*Lux alba*," repeats Alondra. "Under the dark and cold night, remember the warmth of this circle, sisters, that helps us through winter. We've lost one of our beloved sisters. In memory of Owl-Jay, we shall light her candle. We shall light memorial candles for her sister Beverly and her brother-in-law, Jack, both of whom died in Atlanta. Tonight, we pray that Beverly and Jack make a swift journey to the Summerland. And we pray for blessed days for our beloved sister Owl-Jay. We shall miss Jane dearly. She exits this circle with our best wishes." She looks down for a moment. "I, Falconsong, need all your love in these difficult times. Do I have your love, sisters?"

"Yes, high priestess," many say. And many more say "yes" and nod. Rachel leans over me and touches Alondra's arm.

"Liam," Alondra says very formally. Her face under her hood is flickering in the light of the large bonfire. Her green eyes stare into mine, and it looks a little creepy under her hood. Then she bends down and removes a small stone from a pouch on the wild grass under her chair. "Take my onyx stone." She places the very smooth pitch-black stone into my palm. "Let this be your charm. Let it protect you and allow the light of Selene to fall upon you. Although you are not a witch, you have the blessing of my coven as their leader. And you share *my* magic through this small talisman. All of my magic flows through the stone as if you are one with the high priestess herself."

"Thank you," I say.

"Witness this magic from the Hawthorne coven," Alondra says with a nod, turning back to the group. "*Lux alba*."

"*Lux alba*," they all repeat.

"*Lux tenebris*," Capper says, closing his eyes in concentration again and nodding.

"Before I summon my friends, a word of warning to all of you, sisters: you will see things tonight that may disturb you. If any of you are afraid or don't feel ready, leave. I will not hold it against you. We are not using mandragora. You will have to have the strength to face this with full awareness. With Liam's demon, we won't need the magic herbs. Ironically my friend, Liam, has seen things many of you wouldn't believe."

"Why is that?" says Capper. "Why did you allow him to go with you to Alabama? Many of us want to know. Isn't that why he's affected? Jane said, before she left, that she thought you never should have taken him. She also believed much of the hauntings of her sister and her final crash were due to your magic—your work on that poltergeist in Bentmont."

"*Your* work, Cap," snaps Rachel beside me. "You're the one who loves worshipping the backward pentacle—more than she does."

"What's happened, happened," Alondra says, raising a hand to Rachel. She's trying to keep the peace, even though I think she's disliking the asshole as much as Rachel does. "You agreed with our ceremony for Maybelle in Bentmont, high priest. But I erred bringing Liam to that haunting. I admitted this. Now we're here to put things right."

"Jane was the best of us," Capper says, shaking his head. "She also was the most powerful, next to you. Now Jane's gone. We've lost trust in you. And now you're letting your feelings for this dork become more important than the coven."

"Shut up, Cap," says Rachel, standing up. "You're being a dick. Alondra's got enough going on."

"You were Jane's best friend too," Capper snaps,

remaining seated. "I'd think her leaving would make you mad."

"Sit down, Rachel," says Alondra.

Rachel squints at Capper. Then she turns to Alondra and nods, slowly sitting back down in her chair.

"You all have a right to speak in the circle," Alondra says. Even though it looks like she doesn't want Capper to open his mouth again. I catch Capper rolling his eyes. "I ask for two special guests to come forth. Liam is here because he is haunted. I've asked for support from the leaders of two powerful sister covens. One is from the far corner of the world. The other is from Crescent City. Let us ask for them to reveal themselves and bring forth their magic."

Alondra turns to her house. We all do.

The house is dimly lit. The master bedroom, on the second floor—the room with the bathroom where Alondra applied my stupid makeup—has a giant window over-looking the backyard. It's so dark that, although her bedroom light is off, I can make out lights farther away, inside her hallways. Then she gestures to the house. "*Venite foras. Venite foras.*"

I jump as every single one of the witches repeats the words in eerie perfect unison: *Venite foras. Venite foras.*

I'm not sure what we're waiting for. Then I glimpse fire-light flickering off the white house, to our right. This is the side of the house where I entered when I was tossed out of the backyard last week. Two women emerge holding torches. The cloaks are similar to the black ones, but one is green and the other is blue. The one wearing forest green is dark skinned, bald, and without eyebrows. That's Kenosha. Another is wearing a blue cloak. The cloak is mystical, almost a violet color, like she's wearing the coat of some wizard. She's an older middle-aged woman, pale with long blond hair.

"Witches, rise," Alondra says.

The two walk to the bonfire and add their flames to the fire.

"Yatu, Kenosha," Alondra says, rising and embracing Kenosha. "Yatu, Agnes." She hugs Agnes. "Witches, Kenosha is named Willow by her coven in New Orleans. Thank you for arranging this meeting with Andromeda."

Kenosha nods. Then she recognizes me and says with a smile, "Liam. How are you holding up?"

I shrug. She smiles again, nice as hell.

"Please welcome Willow and Andromeda to the Hawthorne coven," says Alondra to the group. All the witches do what they did for me, telling them their names and repeating Alondra's greeting. "Witches, Agnes goes by her occult name, Andromeda. Her Selene coven is named after the blessed goddess Diana. She's traveled far, all the way from England."

The older woman shakes a few hands but maneuvers around everyone to approach me. She shakes my hand and her bright blue eyes stare into mine. They seem to study me, just like Alondra sometimes does. She stands before me for a long time, searching my face for whatever she's looking for.

"Falconsong," says Agnes to Alondra in a British accent, still staring into my eyes. "I wish we could be meeting under better circumstances. This is the vessel?"

Alondra nods.

"A familiar tiding," says Agnes, finally looking at Alondra, "to be celebrating Yule with the passing of friends while welcoming a new initiate."

"Lee isn't an initiate. He's here for cleansing, not initiation."

Got that right.

"If you say so," Agnes replies with a smirk. Then she sits down with Kenosha, across from the fire, near Capper. All the witches sit down.

Agnes stares at me.

I'm definitely not here for an initiation, I'll tell you that. I make sure to shake my head at her.

"I yield the floor to Willow, the high priestess of the Crescent coven," Alondra says, sitting beside me again. Alondra flashes a grin and touches my leg, as if to reassure me.

Kenosha stands and walks in front of the circle, close to the fire.

My bowels are turning. I'm nervous as hell. Allie told me tonight would be weird. Even if this is all I'm up against, weirdness can already be checked off. Her sisters' black cloaks remind me of court, only the judge is my girlfriend and all the jurors are surrounding a big pyre: a campfire that I'm worried the witches intend to throw me in as their sacrificial *vessel*. What if all the makeup was done to get me ready to be prepared and served, as Capper said? What if Alondra plans to skewer me over the bonfire? Ever see the movie *The Wicker Man*?

"Your revered high priestess brought us here because of a threat to her friend," Kenosha says, gesturing to me. "A demon has possessed him. Both Falconsong and I, and the vessel tonight, were introduced to this demon in a little girl's home. Your powerful leader helped me exorcise the spirit from Winona. But Liam was with us and was possessed there. It's also been determined, through divination by Falconsong herself, that an evil force was involved in the death of Owl-Jay's sister and her husband. As many of you know, there was a car accident in Atlanta. And there were red backwards crosses and pentagrams painted inside the car. Both the mother and father died but, thanks to Selene, their daughter Madison survived. The backward stars have made both Andromeda and me consider that the accident might have, indeed, been caused by an Abaddon witch."

"Is Owl-Jay here?" Kenosha asks Alondra.

"She left my circle," Allie replies. I hear a lot of bitterness in her tone.

"Falconsong sensed," continues Kenosha with a nod, "that the car accident was brought on by a demon spell. There's no proof. But your high priestess is very powerful. I have consulted with Agnes, Afreyea, and many other high priestesses throughout the world. We of the council of witches believe Alondra might be right."

"I hear the roads are iced this time of year in these parts, Willow," Agnes suggests. "It could have been a natural event."

"The proof is in the symbols, sister," objects Alondra.

"Owl-Jay was affected by left-sided magic," Kenosha replies with a nod. "And now, I believe, so is Liam. I can feel it as I stand beside him."

Okay, that's creepy. Maybe that's why Agnes keeps staring at me.

"I've spent all my life searching for this evil," Alondra says. "This coven attests to that. Witness Andromeda, from across the world, sisters, to fight Abaddon. Winona was haunted by a demon, not a ghost. The same ghost that now haunts my—"

"Boyfriend?" asks Capper. "Your love for this geek weakens our coven."

"Liam is a friend, ah-ight, not boyfriend," Alondra snaps. She glances at me in her periphery. I know she's lying.

"He's an outsider that messes up the circle," Capper says.

"He needs our help."

"If he hadn't interrupted our Sabbath, you might have convinced Jane to stay."

"Let our guests speak, Cap," Alondra snaps, finally pissed. "If you hold all these objections, you could have chosen to say them last week. Now you're embarrassing me. If you continue this lack of unity, I'll silence you."

"This is what I'm talking about," Capper says with a nod to Kenosha. He sighs, leans back in his plastic chair, and folds his arms.

Kenosha looks down at me again.

"Liam, the magic that you witness tonight will not be all that different from what we saw in Winona's room. The difference is this is in Alondra's backyard—her home, which is not far from yours. Remember, the demon spirit can enter your mind. Being this close to home, as an outsider, I warn you, the shock might disturb you. I know you want to rid yourself of this demon, and I and the other high priestess are here to help. But Lee, this could hurt you."

"Like I could go nuts?" I ask.

"Like you could lose your fucking senses, mate," says Capper.

"My onyx will help," Alondra says. "I gave him my stone as a talisman to share my power tonight."

"Shining forth your power, high priestess, from your coven is a clever idea, Falconsong," Agnes says with a nod.

"He and I will share power only for this exorcism. But it still might not fully protect him." Alondra takes a big sigh, looking at me, worried. That worries me more. "We're here to help him."

"Which is why you should initiate him," Agnes says. "It is too dangerous otherwise. You have mandragora. Give him mandragora and initiate him as a warlock tonight. It will be more protective than the stone. We will bear witness. Do this before the summoning, and we won't fail in ridding him of this evil."

"We already have a high priest," Alondra says.

I catch Capper shaking his head over that. Many witches witness it, and they look aghast. One gasps. Apparently, this is like a slap in the face to Alondra.

Was Capper always this defiant? Or is this since Jane left? Were they friends? It didn't seem like Jane cared for him much. I suppose all the witches are friends, or family, whether they get along or not.

"Your coven's been through a lot," Agnes says after some silence. "The magic of your stone will help protect him, but initiation into this sacred coven would quickly rid him of the demon. It would be more effective, Falconsong. I think you should initiate him."

Alondra loses her scowl at Capper and gazes at me, looking worried again. I really wish she'd stop doing that.

Well, I shake my head fast. There's no way, no way in hell, or for hell, that I'll let them *initiate* me as a witch, or warlock, tonight—possession or not.

"I won't let anything happen to him," Allie says. "But that includes forcing him into such a big decision tonight. He won't be initiated."

"Well, your high priest is right," Kenosha says. "Your heart could be affecting the circle."

"Everything is about you, Allie," Capper storms. "Even when another high priestess from a founding coven is warning you. The lead witch of the Selene coven gives you advice, and you're too sure of yourself to listen even to her."

"Fuck, Cap, don't suddenly start calling me, *Allie!*" Alondra snaps. I jump in response to her outburst. "Don't go there!" Capper lurches back, looking terrified by her sudden outburst. It's the first time I've seen how scared he is of her. "I know what you mean by that name! You call me that again and I'll throw you out of my yard!" She turns to Agnes and shakes her head. "No. He won't be initiated tonight. No, Agnes. No."

Agnes nods.

"Before we begin, did you bring the ancient grimoire of my Crescent coven?" Kenosha asks Alondra. "I promised Agnes I'd show Escoba's book to her."

Alondra nods. She gets a book from under her chair. It's the same one she kept reading in Winona's house. I've seen her jot things down here and there, but she's never shared any of it. It's as occult as her coven.

"May I?" Agnes asks, opening her eyes wide.

Kenosha walks around the fire and hands Agnes the book.

"Is it truly from your founder?" Agnes asks Kenosha, glancing at some pages of the old book.

"It's Escoba's," Kenosha interjects with a nod. "It's genuine."

"I found it in my ancestor's house," Alondra says. "It was in the basement of the Billington House. It is Escoba's grimoire. I use it for my Book of Shadows and for her ancient incantations. It holds more power than any book I've ever known."

"Indeed, Escoba was a powerful witch, they say," Agnes says, running her fingers a few more times along the old leather cover in wonder. She's so careful and awestruck, it's as if Alondra handed her the Hope Diamond or something. "And Kenosha, your circle must be jealous that your coven's grimoire ended up in Hawthorne."

"Yes, Andromeda," Kenosha says with a smile and a nod. "It's actually how Alondra and I became friends."

"You titled it *Broomstick*?" Agnes asks with a laugh. "I doubt the great Escoba Hawthorne came up with that. That rings of your wit, Alondra."

"I did, sister," Alondra says with a chuckle.

"No initiation, then," Agnes says with a nod. But she's still perusing the pages of the book. "So be it. Carry on, Willow."

"Everyone hold hands," says Kenosha, closing her eyes, with a deep breath.

Everyone in white chairs circling the fire holds hands. Kenosha doesn't. She remains standing in front of me. Then she turns her back to me and raises her arms before the fire, like Alondra did during that first ceremony on Hilltop Bluff.

"Spiritus. Spiritus come forth. I speak the ancient tongue: *Ekimmu. Ekimmu. Venite Foras. Spiritus. Venite Foras. Spiritus. Spiritus.*"

At first, Kenosha repeats that over and over again. Then the words are more felt than heard. Some of the other witches, with their heads bowed, repeat it with her. A wind picks up, brushing along the leaves of the wild grass and nearby trees. Pretty soon all the witches except me are repeating the words in unison.

Venite Foras. Spiritus. Venite Foras. Ekimmu.

One of the witches in black cloaks, Beth, gets up and reaches out for me. Alondra cracks open an eye and nods. Rachel stands up and grabs my other hand. Then, as the words are repeated, they move me and my white plastic chair back even farther from the fire and the witch circle. I realize this is a physical representation of me residing outside their coven. Beth gestures for me to sit. Then Rachel takes out a plastic bag that was near her chair and starts pouring a white chalky substance around me and my chair.

"May the demon be cleansed in ash!" Kenosha says, cocking her head back at me. "May it come forth in beltane and leave this vessel."

She takes out a clay figurine. She stands, removes what looks like colored feathers from her cloak, and uses it to brush the figure in her other hand. Then she throws the figurine in the flames and shouts, with wide, wild eyes, "*Igni! Igni! Igni!*" The fire explodes and rises to nearly double its size.

I jump as the whole group of witches scream. It reminds me of the demon's yell itself.

In the clear sky, there is thunder. Everyone's body jerks from the sound—except Alondra. Alondra is completely still, with her head down. Lightning strikes the bonfire. In the flash of light, I clearly see the trees around Alondra's backyard. It strikes me for the first time that her grassy backyard with the surrounding trees feels like a natural shrine.

"*Igni!*" says Kenosha again to the bonfire. "*Igni! Igni Igni!*"

The fire explodes again. It's so weird to see Kenosha excited. This woman is usually so calm. To see her crazed is scary as hell.

I hear more screaming. But I don't think it's from any of the witches. I hear the screams echoing from the trees around me. It reminds me of the ghosts I heard in the walls of the homes we visited. It quickly becomes dark and stormy.

"*Venite foras. Venite foras.*" But these words are Alondra's, and they are said separate from Kenosha and the surrounding witches. "Come forth, Ekimmu. Show your source to me and my sisters. Come out of the vessel, and show us the perpetrator. *Proditor. Proditor. Proditor. Venite foras.*"

Agnes flashes a curious glance at Alondra. As Kenosha bobs up and down, dancing by the fire, the other witches raise their heads and cry with her. But not Alondra. Alondra calmly crouches down in concentration. And, strangely, Agnes is fixated on Alondra now.

It hails. The bonfire changes color from yellow-red to green. It's freezing cold and I clutch my arms around myself.

Then I realize, bizarrely, that the icy storm is not hitting me. Rather, ice and steam are rising from around my chair and seemingly being sucked into the air and back down into the green bonfire.

The green bonfire is now a quarter its size. There is more thunder. Then, after another lightning strike, I jump, witnessing my lanky demon. He's standing in the center of the short green fire before all of us. The thin spirit towers, straight and transparent, over the green flames like a totem. Kenosha is dipping up and down in dance before the spirit, looking as if she is worshipping the specter. The creature is taller than ever, like three stories high, armless, without a face.

There's another scream, but this one is inhuman. It sounds like the scream in my dream, and it seems to be coming from the Ekimmu. It's so loud that many of the witches cover their ears, all except Alondra. Everyone except Alondra and, oddly, me. It's not that loud to me. But everyone else covers their ears, even Kenosha.

Alondra says calmly, with her head dipped down: "*Venite foras.* Come forth, Ekimmu. Come out of the vessel. Reveal what Liam witnessed. Show us the Abaddon witch that moved the spirit into him."

All turns pitch dark ...

I open my eyes in a dimly lit room of a house. I recognize the hallway of Winona's house. I don't know how I got here. I'm seeing the familiar white walls, but the room I face is dark with a large bed.

Now I find myself sitting on the bed. The drapes are shut and only a sliver of yellow light from a partially open door lights the room.

A girl in a witch cloak approaches me from the doorway, crawling on her elbows and knees, reminding me of a spider. Her eyes are pearly white. When beside me, she runs feathers gently along my feet and legs, then over my knees and up to my bare chest and stomach. I don't have my shirt on. She brushes my cheeks. She dances before me, shaking a rattle while brushing the feathers over my body. I can't place who this witch is in the shadows. Then she cradles my head and whispers in my ear.

"Liam. Shh. It's okay, Liam. Enter. *Iugo. Iugo. Iugo.* Leave Winona and enter him now, Ekimmu."

I recognize her voice. It's Kenosha. She crouches close, running her fingers and the feathers up and down my body and on my bare chest. Then I hear her rattle. It is the same rattle I just saw her waving before the bonfire. The witch looks into my eyes with those creepy white eyes.

She puts her arms around my neck. Then she straddles me, dancing over me.

"Enter Liam," Kenosha says beside my ears. "Shh. It's okay. Enter. Shh." She strokes my cheek, then brushes her fingers along my legs. "Join Liam. Join him. Ekimmu iugo. Iugo. Iugo. Ekimmu. Shh, Liam. Ekimmu iugo."

"*Lee! Lee! Not you!*" It's Alondra's voice, but it seems far away.

I don't see Kenosha. I see a pitch-black cloaked figure crouched into a ball. The witch's head is buried in her black cloak in the center of the dark room.

"*You touch him!*" cries Alondra with her head still covered by the hood of her cloak. "*I'll tear you limb from limb! Damn you, Willow!*"

~

"*Vade retro!*" cries Kenosha. "*Igni! Igni! Igni!*"

My eyes open. Kenosha is still dancing, bobbing up and down, before the green fire. But none of the other witches are moving anymore. The hail's stopped. The wind is stilled. Only Kenosha is dancing up and down before the short green bonfire. I think it's the lack of movement around Kenosha that makes her finally turn and look at us. She looks as confused as I feel.

The image of the demon fades. The green fire turns yellowish red. It looks like a normal bonfire. Then everything becomes normal and silent—too silent. The clouds disperse. The moon and stars are out in the clear sky. I hear only the crackling fire. Alondra's yard becomes "normal." That's weirder, in a way.

All the black-cloaked witches of the coven except Capper glare at Kenosha. But no one's talking. Even Agnes is glaring at Kenosha now.

And yet, in the silence, only a single solitary voice is still heard. Alondra's. Strangely, Allie's quietly repeating "*venite foras. Venite foras. Venite foras.* Glory be to Hecate, the conjurer is now revealed."

She stops and looks up at Kenosha.

"You've revealed yourself to my Hawthorne coven, Abaddon witch," Alondra says. She shakes her head violently. "I...I had my suspicions, but I couldn't believe you, my friend, would betray me. As you got rid of your devil, the devil you yourself planted in a little girl, I used the magic of my circle to reveal your spell. And..." She stands up and points her extended arm at Kenosha. I jump back because I notice Allie's eyes are pearly white like Kenosha's in the vision. "I never would have thought it'd be you. Admit your guilt. You planted the demon in Liam. Why? Why would you do such a thing to him?"

All the black-cloaked witches of the Hawthorne coven

get up and stand next to Alondra. Kenosha walks back, nearly tripping and falling into the flames.

"*Abaddon. Abaddon. Abaddon.*" The witches spit, over and over, heckling her and pushing her closer to the fire. "*Abaddon. Abaddon. Abaddon.*" They chant in perfect unison, as if in a trance. I can't help but think it's Allie's magic making them say the words.

Everyone wants to hurt Kenosha. Even Agnes, the only one sitting, looks upset. Honestly, I want to hurt her too. It was her fault. All of it. I can't believe she did this to me. Why? Why would such a sweet girl do such a horrible thing?

I try to escape my chalk circle. But I can't. I find that I can't move beyond the chalk. There's an invisible wall of air stopping me.

"She planted it!" Rachel cries, pointing. "It was her fault!"

"She's the evil one!" says Beth. "She's Abaddon!"

"Did you kill Owl-Jay's sister?" Alondra asks in an unsettlingly calm voice. She sits back down in her white chair and folds her arms, but her eyes are still white.

"I didn't touch Jane's sister," Kenosha replies quickly, shaking her head. Her eyes are bulging at all the witches surrounding her. "She left of her own accord. She knew what you've become. You're Abaddon, Alondra, not me. I had to do this to bring Agnes. You might have shown them my spell, but she will bear witness to the true source of the backward pentacle. You. You're the Abaddon witch. You're to blame for summoning the demon from the ground in the first place."

"How can you accuse me after what you've done!"

All the witches circle Kenosha. Agnes walks in front of Kenosha, defending her.

"Do you protect her?" Alondra asks Agnes. "You

witnessed my vision? Are you also involved? Are you an Abaddon witch too?"

"Back away from her," Agnes says to everyone. She shakes her head. "I didn't know Kenosha did that, Alondra. I was called in to help. But Kenosha showed me evidence of your left-sided magic. Your coven has turned, and I came here to pass judgment. I have evidence. So did Owl-Jay. That's why she left you. And we in the council believe the evil and the origin of the demon itself is from your practices here in Hawthorne."

"We should force the truth from *you*, Allie," says Capper, standing with Agnes. "You're a devil worshipper."

"You fucking hypocrite!" snaps Alondra. "You partook in the same rites, Cap!"

"You're the evil witch you've been searching for all along," Capper says, shaking his head. "I think *you* killed Jane's sister. Jane and I believe that. Your magic killed them. Why do you think she's not here?"

"Yeah? You think that? Well, you're next!"

"I suggest you stand down," Kenosha says. "With your high priest abandoning you, we bind you. You are the Abaddon witch. The demon came from you. I simply brought him here to get Andromeda to help us. Now she's here to pass judgment and excise you from *your* black magic, Alondra."

Kenosha talks bravely, but her eyes are fitful, staring at all the black-cloaked witches surrounding her.

"So this is what this was about?" Alondra snaps at Kenosha. "You summoned a demon into a little girl. Then transferred him to my boyfriend to convince Agnes to come to the States? How could you do that to a little girl? You claim I'm the one whose magic should be bound? What about what you did to Winona? I've never done anything so evil!"

"I didn't haunt Winona," Kenosha says, shaking her head. "Something else put the demon into her. We believe it came to her when you called on the devil god to rid Alice and Maybelle of the poltergeist. You used black magic and cursed Owl-Jay. And that transferred as blowback to her sister."

"Your champion, Andromeda, isn't even convinced that car accident was magic!" objects Alondra. "And Jane fought with me, but even she never accused me of killing her sister."

"Then why isn't she here, *Allie*?" asks Capper.

"I can't believe this," Alondra says. Then she turns to Agnes. "How can you believe I'm the one being evil when Kenosha planted a demon in a little child? And then in my friend!"

"I transferred the spirit from the child, yes," says Kenosha, "but I never planted it. And I knew I could take it out of Liam tonight. And we have. It was the only way for Agnes to meet with Capper and bind you."

"You're here to bind me!" Alondra finally gets up. "I'll fucking bind you!"

Her crowd of black-cloaked witches are at it again.

Abaddon. Abaddon. Abaddon.

Only this time, they're looking at Agnes and Capper too. Agnes stares at the witches surrounding her. As wise and confident as this witch was when she first arrived, her eyes are now turning nervously about her like Kenosha's.

"Kenosha has shown me evidence of black magic in your rites," says Agnes, shaking her head. "This demands an investigation, Alondra. A temporary binding from black magic should be done with your coven in Hawthorne."

"What I do in my backyard, old woman, is none of your fucking business," cries Alondra. "You're a hypocrite. You two are more into the backward pentacle than we are."

"She's becoming dangerous, Agnes," Kenosha says, shaking her head.

"First you plant a possession in Liam," says Alondra, walking up so she and Kenosha are face to face. "Now you dare to challenge my power in my own backyard! My hallowed ground! How dare you!"

"Don't do this, Alondra," warns Kenosha, shaking her head. "With Agnes, and without Capper, you won't win."

Kenosha falls to the ground. It looks like Alondra pushed her, but I didn't see her lay a hand on her. Kenosha starts shaking on the ground as if she's seizing.

"Stop it!" cries Agnes, putting her hand up. She falls on her knees beside Kenosha. "We can investigate both of you. Just stop, Alondra! If you attack her, I'll side with her."

Alondra folds her arms. Then her whole group of witches huddles around Agnes and Kenosha, shouting obscenities at them. Again, the group seems to act out Alondra's thoughts and emotions, as if they are controlled by her. Some of the witches try to grab Kenosha, but Capper pushes them away.

I press against my "wall" of air. I can feel something blocking my hands. Then, like a mime, I run my palms along this bizarre air-boundary.

Some of the white dust scuffs under my tennis shoe. I can move my feet beyond the circle of chalk! Quickly, I brush the dust away from my chalk circle.

"Move out of my way, Cap," says Alondra. "You too, Agnes. This is personal now between me and my so-called *friend*."

"Are you going to kill her?" asks Capper.

"You saw what Kenosha did, sisters, didn't you?" Alondra asks, cocking her head back at the group, ignoring him.

"Yes," they all say in perfect unison.

"Stand down, Falconsong," says Agnes, shaking her

head, looking at all the surrounding witches. "Your coven is without a high priest. You can't win, hallowed ground or not."

Alondra stares at Kenosha. Kenosha is on her knees, grasping her head tightly. "Get out of my head!" I hear the noise. It's that machine-like noise I heard at my first haunting. But it's barely audible. Somehow, it's deafening to Kenosha. She's writhing on the floor, and Agnes is trying to help her.

"You've taken my high priest? Thought of everything, did you?" Alondra is glaring down, with eerie pearly-white eyes, at Kenosha. "Did you forget I possess your power with your coven's magic book?"

Kenosha can't answer. She's clutching her ears.

"This triumvirate binds you!" shouts Agnes, looking up and still holding Kenosha. "Your own high priest and I excise your black magic from Hawthorne! I relinquish your power, Alondra, and your leadership under Hecate. You have no power under Selene anymore."

"I fucking hate you," Alondra replies, looking down on Agnes. "I think I've always hated you. Your powerless friends couldn't help my parents. You make rules that only you can break. And you accuse me of evil, when you are far worse. It seems I've found our Abaddon witches, sisters."

"No witch killed your parents," says Kenosha, shaking her head, still gripping it with her hands. "I'm your friend. This is all part of your delusion."

I step out of the circle. I'm free!

But I'm not stupid enough to join the mob.

Alondra cocks her head back and looks at me. She notices I'm free and manages to flash me a very sinister smile. That makes me shudder. I know my girlfriend well enough to know what she's capable of when angry.

But Allie walks away from the two high priestesses and

crouches down alone on the grass. Kenosha stops squirming. Then Alondra curls herself into a ball like she did in Winona's room.

"She's casting!" says Kenosha in Agnes's arms. "Chant the words sister, quickly. Say the words with us, high priest. Bind her. Quick. *Relinque*." The three echo the words and point at Alondra. "*Relinque. Relinque. Relinque. Falconsong.*"

Alondra doesn't respond. Instead she sits cross-legged and buries her head further in her lap.

"*Relinque. Relinque. Relinque.*"

The three of them whisper it repeatedly before the mob of black-cloaked witches. The witches, oddly, turn from them and sit back down in their chairs around the fire.

Alondra rebukes quietly, "*Invocare. Invocare.*" She says it like a whisper, but it echoes through the air.

"*Relinque. Relinque. Relinque.*"

"Invocare Escoba," Alondra says quietly. "Invocare. Escoba, I call on you, Escoba Hawthorne, to rid me of these vipers on my hallowed ground. Send Willow to Sheol where she fucking belongs."

"My god!" shrieks Kenosha, pointing. "Agnes, she's got the book again. Get my grimoire, Capper! Hurry!"

"But she has no high priest?" says Capper, shaking his head.

"That's her coven's grimoire!" cries Agnes. "She has her coven's power and hers. Escoba's! *Grab it, Capper!*"

Kenosha's eyes are bulging. Alondra is kneeling on her grimoire—the book she called *Broomstick*.

Invocare Escoba. Invocare, Invocare, Invocare.

Alondra is still. It's weird, but she seems more frightening like this than when she was shouting. Her face is buried in her lap, but she keeps quietly chanting.

Agnes tries wielding a small leather pouch in her palm,

shaking it toward Alondra. She cries, "*Avra kehdabra. Falcon-song. Relinque.*" Nothing happens.

Capper charges Alondra. I tackle him to the ground. He's a big guy, and he rolls with me on the grass, pinning my arms. I manage to twist and turn Capper around, freeing a hand. Then I deck him really hard in the face. He knees my leg, aiming for my groin. He grabs me and yanks me up, ready to hit me again. I slug him instead.

"*Prohibe,*" Alondra whispers. "*Prohibe. Proditor.*"

Capper falls to the ground before me, shaking as if in a seizure. Then he lies completely still, frozen. I raise my hand over him. His eyes follow, but he doesn't appear to be able to move his head. His stillness makes my last punch vicious. It knocks him out.

"They brought you to America to witness Abaddon, Agnes," says Alondra quietly. "Witness her evil. There she is. Watch me take the devil and cast her down into perdition upon my sacred hallowed ground."

Kenosha can't speak. She's clutching her head and rolling on the grass again.

"Stop it!" cries Agnes. "Stop it, Alondra! You're hurting her."

"*Abaddon, Abaddon, Abaddon,*" All the witches cry at Agnes, circling the fire.

"Gather them up, sisters," Alondra commands calmly, as she stands up. She holds her book under her arm. "Gather them. Your former high wizard, Capper, too. Let Escoba take care of all of them."

The wind has picked up again. And then comes hail once more. The ice sizzles as it falls upon the ever-growing red bonfire.

I run to Alondra.

"*Invocare. Invocare Escoba,*" Alondra says quietly, looking down.

"Allie, what are you doing?"

"*Invocare. Invocare.*"

"Allie. What are you doing!"

"Ask Kenosha." Allie looks up with those creepy white eyes. But she's not looking at me. She has her head turned back to the house. "She planted evil in you. Ask her what she deserves."

"Look!" cries one of the witches. She's pointing to the house. A dark-skinned witch carrying a torch is walking from the left side of the house to the bonfire. She's wearing a black cloak with a yellow-and-black head wrap. In the shadows, the cloak doesn't look all that different from ours. But I can see the house through her body.

"Welcome Escoba Hawthorne, sisters," Alondra says with a grin, made only more perverse under her pearly-white eyes. "We hail a special guest tonight. Escoba Hawthorne, welcome, welcome to my home."

"Stop it." I grab Alondra's arm. "Stop it! It's enough, Allie. Stop this."

Alondra looks at me. Her white eyes and twitchy lips and eyelids are quite terrifying. I'm remembering Winona screaming at this sight.

"She possessed you with a demon, Liam," Alondra says to me. "You don't want her punished?"

"What are you going to do to her? To them?"

"Make her pay." Alondra shrugs and looks back at Kenosha, who seems to cry out even more in pain. "Make all the Abaddon witches pay."

Agnes falls to the ground, shaking, beside Kenosha.

The ghost-witch approaches the fire. Escoba raises both her arms to the air, facing the flames. A cry is heard similar to that of the demon. Then white lights like the orbs I saw at Winona's quickly encircle the flames. The orbs fly around the flames and then stretch, looking more like glowing white sheets.

Kenosha is dragged, like I was once, by an invisible force, toward the trees. But this time I see the white streaks from the fire, in the shadows, tugging at her. Agnes recovers enough to rush to her, but a few of the black-cloaked witches jump from their chairs and hold her back.

"Alondra, what are you doing!" I shout.

She simply watches with her arms folded as the spirits carry Kenosha, in the darkness, toward a large tree.

"Alondra, what's going to happen to her?"

By the tree, Kenosha is being tugged into the ground. Grass and dirt are kicked up as her body is thrust again and again into the soil. Then branches come down and hold her. Her screams are cries of pain. It sounds like the ghosts are tearing her flesh and breaking her bones to plunge her into the ground.

"Help her," I say to Alondra. "Stop hurting her, Allie. Help her."

"You're such an angel, Liam," Alondra says with a grin.

"And you're evil. You're hurting her."

I snatch Alondra's book from under her arm. Allie's eyes immediately change back from white to green in the light of the bonfire. She nearly falls over, as if I struck her. Escoba vanishes. Then all her black-cloaked witches spin around and start shouting at me.

Kenosha is panting, kneeling by the tree. The branches have returned to their former places. But Kenosha's face and body are covered with mud and grime. The clouds disperse and moonlight shines forth in a clear evening sky.

Alondra squints at me. A few witches drop to their knees crying, apparently breaking out of their trance and in complete shock over everything that's happened.

"Give me my book!" Alondra shouts at me.

She grabs for it, but I bat her hand away.

"Give me back my fucking book, Liam!"

She shoves me to the ground. I shake my head.

"That's my book!" Alondra says, shaking her head violently. "Give me back *Broomstick!*"

I get up. She reaches for it again. I push her away.

Agnes runs to Kenosha and helps her up.

"Fuck! Give me back my book, Lee!" Alondra screams at me with wide-open green eyes. "What are you doing!"

"You were going to kill her!"

"She was going to kill me!" she cries, jumping up. "She possessed you! She was going to take away my power. Witchcraft is everything to me. You know that."

"Yes. Everything. Over me. Over everyone. Even your friend Jane."

"The stone," says Agnes, wide-eyed, supporting Kenosha. "He has her stone. Lee, she can't touch you with the black stone! Don't give her back the book. Give it to us. You saw what she was going to do with it."

"*Give me back my fucking book!*" cries Alondra, trying to grab for it again. "I warn you." This isn't the possessed Alondra with white eyes. She's simply pissed.

"No."

"You gonna give it to them?" Alondra asks, gesturing to Agnes and Kenosha. "Huh? They were going to take away my power. I've spent my whole life learning witchcraft. More than any of those so-called leaders. I've helped save so many souls. You saw the girls I helped. You witnessed everything. Then she possessed you with a demon. I showed you. So you want to give the witch that possessed you my power? They came to take it away from me because they were afraid of me. I've become too powerful, they say. They don't give a shit who or what I worship. They just don't like seeing a witch more powerful than they are. I don't worship the devil, that fucking hypocrite Capper does. And they do too, if you want to know the truth."

"You almost killed her. I believe them. And I believe Jane. You...you are becoming evil, Alondra."

The two head witches come closer, cautiously. So does Capper, though he still looks hurt by my fist. Most of the witches of the coven have approached—those that aren't in shock, weeping, on the ground. But they're all keeping their distance, staring at the magical book under my arm. I'm holding it tightly while running my other hand over the stone in my pocket.

"Give it to me, Liam," says Agnes. "I knew her parents. My Selene coven can guard Escoba's grimoire."

"Great good you did for them!" snaps Alondra, cocking her head back.

"We can care for the book without causing harm," says Agnes.

"No," I say, shaking my head. "I'll keep it from all of you. None of you shall have it."

"*That's my book!*" cries Alondra in a high-pitched scream. "What are you talking about? What are you going to do with it? You're not even a fucking warlock! Damn you, Lee, hand me Escoba's grimoire. Now! It's mine!"

I shake my head.

"Are you serious?" She's searching my eyes, while still trying to snatch it from my grasp.

I nod.

"Fuck off then!" Alondra shouts. She gestures to the front of the house. "Get out! I was punishing Kenosha, and punishing her rightly, for me, and *for you*, Liam. But you want to stick your nose in shit you don't understand? I tried to help you, and you repay me by taking away everything I've lived for!"

"Lee, hand us the book," Kenosha says. "Please. It's my

coven's book. I knew I could bring my sister here if I possessed you. It was to stop Alondra, not to hurt you. We don't worship the backward pentacle like she does."

"Lamia!" says Alondra. "You lamias. You don't distinguish between good or evil if it empowers you."

"I wasn't going to hurt her or you, Liam," Kenosha says. "She was going to hurt me." She's back to being the calm, collected Kenosha I remember. But her face is coated in mud and grime. Her calm is deceitful. Evil. "You saw the Abaddon witch for yourself, Lee."

"You put a ghost in me," I say. "You tricked me." I shake my head. "No, I won't give it to you either. But you two leave her alone. Leave her be or I'll hand the book back to her."

Agnes nods sadly. "The council accepts this."

"I don't care what you or your stupid council accepts!" shouts Alondra. "*Get out of my house!*" She whirls at me again. "*Hand me my fucking book, Liam!* Now. It's not yours! None of this is your business."

"I have your word that you won't give it to Alondra if we leave?" asks Agnes. "I can trust you?"

I nod.

Kenosha turns to Agnes. "I know his heart to be true, Andromeda. He will keep his promise."

"So be it," Agnes says with a nod. "Hide it from her. And us, if you must. You're protected until the morning by her stone. But beware, Liam, for tomorrow you no longer have protection from the Hawthorne witch."

"Get out of my house!" snaps Alondra at them again.

Agnes joins Kenosha and Capper and they walk out of the backyard.

"*LAMIA,*" Alondra shouts at them again, whatever that means.

Then Alondra whirls back to me. She walks right up to my face and searches it. In love, I was aroused when she met my gaze like this. In rage, it's repulsive. "You're nothing to me, ah-ight? If you don't give me what's mine, I will never speak to you again."

"I can't. You were going to kill her."

"Damn you, I'm not a murderer. I'm a witch. I was going to hurt her like she hurt you. I had every right. But you'll never understand me, will you? You'll never understand what we are. We're witches. You're not a witch and you're not a man. And now you're taking something that doesn't belong to you. Well, get this." She digs her finger into my chest. "I hate you. I hate you as much as I hate them."

"Witchcraft is the only thing you ever cared about."

"Don't ever come near me again."

She turns her back on me. Then she walks over to a few witches who are sitting in the grass, with their heads in their hands, crying. She sits down by one of her sisters, puts her arm around her, and whispers something.

I leave. I walk to the side yard with the book tucked under my arm.

A few of the other witches shout "Abaddon" at me. *At me.* That's how crazy they are. I hear one of them—Beth, I think —yell for Alondra to run after me and fight for the book. She doesn't. But, as I go, I feel their stares.

I throw the book on the passenger seat when I get into my car. I feel tears in my eyes. I never cry. But I whimper. I don't think I've done that since I was a little boy.

I feel so sad.

No, I'm mad. I'm furious. I practically became a witch for her. But when it came down to witches or me, again, her witchcraft was more important.

I throw the sunshade down and look into the mirror under the cabin light. I still have that stupid makeup on my face. I start rubbing it hard with the back of my hand to try to smear it off.

Where will I go? If I'm not a witch, I'm no one in Hawthorne. I don't belong with the coven. And I don't belong with Alondra. I never did. I should have left that night I wandered Hilltop Bluff.

I always liked how calm and self-assured Alondra appeared. That was part of my attraction, I think. Now all I can hear is her shouting and belittling me. And for the first time since I met her, I truly feel like she's a witch. Not a witch like Glinda, a wicked witch.

I fell in love with a witch. Now the crush is over. And I want to leave Hawthorne forever.

22

A TIKI BAR

"I want out of Hawthorne," I say, sucking Coke from a straw.

"That's what you said last time," says Bill.

I look around. I'm in a Tiki bar, with dried palm leaves and bamboo and a large island mural along the wall, making the restaurant feel like a tropical island. We're in the same restaurant at Myrtle Beach as last time, only the patio outside is closed due to storms. In fact, it's raining outside. That'll be fun driving back.

"Merry Christmas," Bill says with a toast, drinking some beer.

"Happy Yule," I grunt.

"You sounded like shit on the phone. I only wish I could get you a beer. That waitress…" He points to a blond waitress at the bar counter. "Is watching us like a hawk this time."

I shrug.

"Don't be so depressed, bud. I warned you. You'll find another girl."

"I really liked her, Bill. She was different."

Of course, I told Bill all about the exorcism. He didn't

believe a word of it. I guess the sex and pentagram were believable enough, but flying white wraiths and magical books were a bit too much.

"You think I can transfer to Duke?" I ask.

"If that's what you want. You have the grades and test scores. And Hawthorne's a really good school. I can see what I can do."

"And no witches."

"No bitches," Bill says, raising his glass with a nod. "All girls are witches, you know."

"That's not true," I say. My voice sounds so down I'm depressing myself.

He shrugs.

I look up and there's a Falcons game on a TV hanging near the bar. They're playing the Rams. Of course, baseball season, my favorite, is over. And I'm not much of a football fan.

"How's the dissertation?" I ask.

Bill just shrugs.

"You guys want dessert?" asks the blond waitress. And wouldn't you know it, she's the same waitress as last time. I don't think she recognizes me.

Bill raises his brow to me. I shake my head.

"You want another *Coke*?"

I look up and she has a way-too-wide grin. Yep, she recognizes me.

I shake my head and Bill chuckles as she walks off. "Bitches. They are all bitches, Lee. As soon as you realize that's what women are, you won't be upset when a fling doesn't work out. Just get to know them on a superficial level, like me. That way they can't get under your skin."

"It's weird because I still want her."

"You fell for her, bud. Look." He leans forward and takes off his glasses. Bill's wearing his glasses instead of contacts today. They're a bit nerdy. "Why don't you stay in Hawthorne for a little while longer. Try the next semester. They have a good psychology program. You can just ignore these goth freaks and live your own life."

"You can't help me with Duke?"

"I can try. Like I said, you have the grades and the scores."

"Do what you can, Bill."

He nods. Then he looks up at the football game and sips his beer.

"You probably should stay the night," he says. "The roads are slick and dangerous. You can stay over if you want. Then we can go together tomorrow."

"I really don't care."

The waitress hands my friend the bill. I grab for it, but he presses it against his chest. He shakes his head.

"When you make money, Lee."

"Fine. And thanks for meeting."

"I don't mind, bud. You're the one driving six hours. I just wish the patio was open today and I could have gotten you a beer."

23

TRICK OR TREAT

I'M PACKING. THIS IS THE PERFECT TIME TO LEAVE. ALL MY finals are done. The semester of conjuring and weirdness is finally over. In fact, most of the students are gone. The hallway by my dorm is empty.

If things had worked out, Allie and I might have spent time together this week. No, I know we would have. We're the only ones not too close to family. I'm sure I probably would have just stayed at her house.

Well, things didn't work out, Liam, did they?

I stuff a sweater in a duffel bag. Then I'm throwing socks in the side pocket. Yeah, the whole thing's a bit depressing.

I have a quick method of packing. I like to open a box, lean it close to the dresser or desk, and dump the stuff in the box. Easy and fast. That's the advantage to traveling by car. I don't know what I'd do if I were flying. See, I've got enough room in my car to fit the whole dorm room.

I look at the upper bunk. I bet if I stayed they still wouldn't find a replacement roommate. I wonder what happened to the first one? Maybe he was abducted by a witch?

I drop the books, one by one, into a cardboard box. Then I look outside and see what I dread out the window. Snow. And it's not just a little; it's falling like sheets and I can barely make out the outside. In fact, though it's afternoon, it's dark and cloudy.

There's a knock on my door.

You thinking what I'm thinking? Alondra? Well, I've guessed that about ten times now over the past week. It's never her. Anyway, I think she was pretty clear with her last words. It's always a dorm neighbor or my resident assistant.

I open the door. It's neither. It's Bill.

"Great weather we're having, Lee. I'm so happy I promised to help you pack this morning."

"You're back early. I said around two."

"Yeah." He looks out the window and shakes his head. "Well, I don't think we're going anywhere anyway. We should spend the night in a hotel. If they have hotels here." Then he puts his hand over his forehead and squints at the window, scoping out the area outside. Of course, there's nothing to see but white. "Where the hell's all those witches you were telling me about, anyway?"

I chuckle. "They always come when you least expect it. If you want, you can take the top bunk. We could stay here and leave tomorrow morning."

"I guess. Might be fun being in college again."

He brushes some frost from the glass and peers out again. I pack more shirts.

"Empty," he says, staring out at the snow. Then he says quietly, "Nope, no witches. All them witches—"

He freezes. I look to see what's going on. He's staring at the door.

"I...guess I found one," Bill says with a smile.

There, standing by the threshold, is a black-cloaked witch. She's weirdly wearing her full witch getup with full-on goth makeup. She even has a black star on her forehead. And she has bright green eyes.

"Hi," the witch says with a wave.

"My name's Bill." He walks up to her and shakes her hand. "Bill Reardon."

She doesn't really look at him. She's staring at me.

"Going somewhere?" Alondra asks me.

"Yeah," I say with a nod, raising my brow. "Home. This is Bill. You guys might get along pretty well. He studies the occult. Supernatural. Ghosts. And witches. He's a graduate student and teacher at Duke."

"Professor Reardon," she says, nodding again.

"Yeah," he says with a nod and a sigh. Then he turns to me. "Listen, Liam. Why don't I bring some of these boxes to the car? You can meet me—"

But I'm already carrying a box past him. I completely ignore Alondra. Bill grabs a box and rushes behind, trailing me.

"Uh," he says, rushing beside me. "That looked like a witch, Lee. I'm guessing that was your friend?"

I don't respond. Then I grip the box with one arm and somehow manage to push the glass door of our dormitory open. I regret it. It's freezing cold and the snow is covering the ground. It makes me think of Alondra. She wasn't wearing a coat. Then I inwardly curse myself for giving a shit.

"Liam, I know you're upset. But it seems your girlfriend wants to talk."

"She's not my girlfriend."

"Well, seeing her is probably making you feel worse. But, man, you're not going anywhere in this weather. No one is. It's not just your car. Not even a snowplow would fare well tonight."

We're standing outside, by the door, in the freezing cold.

And it's weird. We could easily turn back, but if we do that we'll be back at my dorm room. And in my room there's little doubt that Alondra is waiting to talk to me. But even though we're frozen, an awning above us is keeping out the snowflakes.

"She probably knew," I say, stomping the ground.

"What?" he asks, turning to me. He takes off his glasses and dries them off with a handkerchief.

"Or maybe she made it snow."

He lifts his brow, probably thinking I'm completely insane.

We stand some more. We can't go to the car because we'll be pummeled with ice. And we can't go back because...

"It's an amazing campus," Bill mutters. From the corner of my eye, I see him nod and stare at the buildings with his hands in his pockets. Then he turns and sees the trees, covered in snow. He just nods. "Beautiful university."

"It's the wilderness."

Bill nods again. He turns to me and just flashes a fake smile. "It's nice. Quiet."

"Quiet? No. It's not quiet."

I know she'll be back there. I know she's probably leaning on the wall by the door. I know her too well. I can picture everything. She'll be waiting, knowing I'll have to return for the rest of the boxes. She probably raised her hands and did some hocus pocus shit and threw ice over the roads.

Or maybe she's not here to talk to me at all. Perhaps this moment of indecision is exactly what Allie needs. Maybe she's rummaging through my private stuff to get the book. That's probably it. She was quite clear in her backyard last week that she hated me.

Well, Alondra, you will never find Broomstick. *Believe me. No matter what trick or treat you plan, there'll be no* Broomstick. *If there are two things I'm good at, it's keeping secrets and hiding things.*

I look at Bill. He's got his hands in his pockets still staring outside. He nods uncomfortably and sighs.

"Stay here," I say in a huff, dropping the box near the door.

And, well, he just nods again.

And then, just as I suspected, Alondra's standing across from the door of my room. She has her head down. But her hood's down too, revealing her long black hair. Her cloak is wet. She must have walked through the snow. Her hair's dry, so she probably had the hood over her head. That must have been an interesting sight. A black-cloaked witch walking through white snowy ice. She probably figured it was too stormy for many people to see. Or maybe she is in the same mood as I am and just really didn't care.

"I...I came for another box," I say.

She looks up and my eyes catch hers. She smiles sadly.

"I won't give you the book," I add.

"I'm not here for the book."

"I don't know if I believe you."

"I didn't come here for your book."

My book?

"I...Liam, I fucked up. I fucked up real bad."

"Hey, don't use profanity to make yourself look cool or bad. Don't say things to try to attract me to you."

"I am bad, Lee. But you're not." She shrugs. "That's why I love you so much. You're my guardian angel. I told you that. You and I are like that CD I gave you that first time we talked in lecture. Like twins. One cherub with wings, one without. You and I—"

"I just want to have a normal college life."

She laughs. I can't believe it, but she is actually laughing at me. "Take a look at my face and clothes. You don't want a normal college life."

"I don't want to talk with you right now," I say, and I open my door. "Excuse me." I walk in knowing full well she's watching. Then I grab another box. It's the heaviest, with my books. "You would have killed her if I didn't stop you."

"That's not true," she says by the door. "I can see that it might have looked like that. But she was being dragged to Sheol. Much of magic is a mix of thought and reality. She couldn't have been trapped in the ground. It was an illusion. But I entered her mind, and it was her illusion too. You see..." She gets close to me and that upsets me. I push her away and make my way down the hall. "Escoba was sending them to Sheol," she continues, walking beside me. "Sheol is like a between world. I was hurting her, not—"

I stop. "You said you hated me. You wanted to make clear...what was it? That I'm not a man. So why would you come to see me?"

"I said that because I did hate you that night. But I went after Kenosha 'cause she went after you. Then you complained about what I was doing and took away what I love. Part of me will never agree with you for that. I'm not saying sorry about my anger over that."

"You were killing her."

"I tell you, I wasn't."

"Why are you here now?"

She sighs. Then she looks into the room. "Can I help you move?"

"Are you serious!" I probe her green eyes and it kills me. I feel that familiar rise in my chest. But it's painful. Because it's over. "Why are you staring at me like that? Are you casting a spell on me?"

"I like looking into your eyes," she says with a chuckle.

"I'm the one who likes your green eyes, okay Allie? You

said you don't like your eyes. We've already been through this."

"I know," she says with a nod, mesmerizing me. "I don't like my eyes. But I like how you look at me when you gaze into mine."

Fuck! I mean...fuck! How can she piss me off so much while making me still feel for her?

"Liam, I'm sorry. I really screwed up. First with Jane, now with you. With Jane, it's irreparable. But with you...they were just the wrong words."

"I can't do this, Alondra," I say, looking down and shaking my head.

The weight of the books is killing my arms. It actually hurts. Like her. I want to head down the rest of the hallway, but something's stopping me. She's stopping me. She's keeping me from leaving. And I hate myself for letting her do it.

"Why are you wearing so much makeup? You heading to another Sabbath tonight?"

"You said I scheme," she says with a shrug. "I wanted to be real with you. I didn't want to screw up anymore. Not with you. I wanted to just be me. This is me. Like when I showed you my house. This is the real me. For you."

"I can't give you back your book."

"I get that."

"And I can't be around anyone who worships the devil. Satanic ceremonies. Pentagrams. I've thought about this all week. You call me an angel. Well, I should have put my foot down when we first met. Otherwise, me being with you was evil. All that stuff has to stop if you want me around you. If I'm to be anywhere near you, I don't want to be around Satan worshipping and stuff."

"Okay."

"What?" I say, moving back. I nearly fall over from the

weight of my books, and she grabs me, stopping me from falling. "What do you mean, *okay*? I didn't say we were making a deal."

"Don't go, Lee," she says, holding my arm. A single tear falls down her cheek. "Please. You're all I have in Hawthorne. Nothing else in this town means anything to me anymore."

"I don't think this is going to work."

I lug the heavy box down the hall and turn toward the exit. I stop for a moment and reposition the heavy box in my arms. I glance over at the glass door. Bill's still standing there with his hands in his pockets, staring at the woods in the cold. And, of course, Alondra is standing right next to me. She's even carrying my backpack on her shoulder, "helping me" move. That's completely ridiculous, but it's so her. I put the box down for a second.

"Give it a chance, Lee," she says with a sigh. "Don't leave like Jane. If it doesn't work, then it doesn't. Nothing's permanent. But trying is still worth it. Isn't it?"

I look at her. She smiles her infamous sweet smile.

"Did those witches take your power? Did I take it by taking your book?"

"No one can do that. The only thing they did to me was dissolve the coven. They did that, for a short while. Capper's gone. Which is ridiculous. He brainwashed them. Capper's more of a left-hand practitioner than I could ever be. Anyway, you know he was overdue to leave." She shrugs. "But they can't take away my witchcraft. Or my circle. I was born a witch and I'll die a witch."

"Do you know who planted the demon in Winona?"

"No," she says. She turns from me. Then she loses her smile and turns very serious, nodding. "I'll keep searching. Kenosha and Agnes are wrong. It wasn't just a fight over me, it was a fight over their beliefs. They're wrong about evil.

There are real Abaddon witches out there. I know it. There is evil. And Lee, I might not be a good witch, but I'm not a bad one. Willow is wrong about me. So is Jane." She turns back to me. "So are you. I'm not a devil. I've helped people. You saw Winona and Melanie after the haunting. And I've helped so many others."

In the silence, a student finally comes rushing down the hallway. He's got a heavy duffel bag and coat slung over his arm. He nods to us and then looks back, staring at Alondra's getup as he runs out the glass door. I see Bill move to the side, but he doesn't look over at Alondra and me.

"Well, I'm still not giving you the book."

"Hmm," she says, cocking her head with a sly smile, checking me out. "You'd be surprised the power of a succubus."

I chuckle despite myself.

She gestures to Bill by the glass door. "Why don't you tell him to go home? I'll help you *unpack*."

"You have to give me some time to think this over."

"Ah-ight. But how 'bout I try something to help you make up your mind."

She puts her arms around me. She doesn't kiss me. See, that wouldn't be Alondra. No, she stares at me, scrutinizing my eyes as if reading my thoughts with her bright green eyes that she hates but she knows I love. She runs her hand over my hair, studying my head. Then her hands touch my arms and my back. She squeezes me tight. Then, after all that, she finally lays her black lips gently over my naked ones.

"I hurt you," she says between kisses, running her hand down my hair. "Kenosha brought the demon but I invited you. It was my fault. I blame myself. I won't hurt you again, Lee. I'd rather hurt myself."

And she kisses me some more, tasting my tongue with hers. There's spearmint there. I smell it and taste it.

And, well, I'm hooked. Again. I even sigh over my personal struggle. She simply kisses me more over that. Somehow, I manage to disengage from her embrace.

"I need to tell him," I say, gesturing to Bill through the glass door. "I don't think he's going to be very happy after driving six hours to help me."

"This is our third fight," she says with a shrug. She rubs my back, hugs me, and leans into my lips again.

"Will you stop kissing me?" I lean back from her mouth.

"I'm trying to color your lips black." She laughs, touching my cheek and lips with her fingers.

"You'll never do it," I say.

"Too bad. But I'm fine with it as long as I can hang with Liam Johansen. Go tell your friend you're staying. But hurry." Then she whispers in my ear, "The lips aren't the only thing black. Remember the lace bra? I'm wearing it. Let me show you how it looks in your dorm room. The best thing about fighting is making up."

She looks at me with a big grin and those gorgeous green eyes. I kiss her some more.

In the back of my mind, I wonder if Bill is watching us. I'm wondering what a guy in a T-shirt and jeans looks like making out with a black-cloaked wicked witch.

THE END

WITCHY ADVENTURES ARE CONTINUED IN THE
NEXT BOOKS IN THE HAWTHORNE UNIVERSITY
WITCH SERIES

THE SERIES

- BROOMSTICK
- WINDSTORM
- THE HAWTHORNE WITCH
- WITCH MIRROR
- RAVENS
- SHADOW CAST

SHORT STORIES AND PREQUELS

- BELTANE FIRE short story prequel (Book 0.5)
- SAMHAIN WITCH (Book 3.5)
- CANDY CRONE (Book 6.5)

THE BOXED SETS

- THE HAWTHORNE UNIVERSITY WITCH
  SERIES (1-3)
- THE HAWTHORNE UNIVERSITY WITCH
  SERIES (4-6)
- THE HAWTHORNE UNIVERSITY WITCH
  HOLIDAY COLLECTION

ALSO BY A.L. HAWKE

PARANORMAL ROMANCE

- THE HAWTHORNE UNIVERSITY WITCH SERIES (I-III)
- THE HAWTHORNE UNIVERSITY WITCH SERIES (4-6)
- THE HAWTHORNE UNIVERSITY WITCH HOLIDAY COLLECTION
- SHADES
- HAUNTING JOY
- PHANTOM MASQUERADE

- MY EVIL EYE
- THE GUARDIAN
- NECTAR OF AMBROSIA
- CORA

FANTASY: THE AZURE SERIES

- HARMONIA
- CORA: RISE OF THE FALLEN GODDESS
- AZURE BLUE
- CORAL RED
- PRINCESS SOJOURN

SCIENCE FICTION

- CANDY SAVANT SERIES

Books available at https://alhawke.com/books

PARTING WORDS

What did you think of *Alondra*? By placing a book review, you can inform others of your thoughts and help spread the word about my book.

Want more? Periodically I like to send news regarding current or new projects. If you'd like to be privy, I encourage you to sign up to my email newsletter. Your information will remain private and you can cancel any time.

Sign up at www.alhawke.com or scan the following QR code:

ACKNOWLEDGMENTS

I want to thank George B. for his beta read. Stephanie Marshall Ward for her copy edit. Stephanie went beyond sentence structure, detailing nuances that improved my story. Alexa helped polish my novel once again with her proofread. And Regina Wamba created a fantastic witchy cover, perfectly capturing my vision on the first take, while maintaining the look of the Hawthorne University trilogy.

And a final big thanks to my readers. Your interest in Hawthorne U drove me to delve deeper into Alondra's past. That was a lot of fun. I hope it was for you.

ABOUT THE AUTHOR

A.L. Hawke is the author of the internationally bestselling Hawthorne University Witch series. The author lives in Southern California torching the midnight candle over lovers against a backdrop of machines, nymphs, magic, spice and mayhem. A.L. Hawke writes fantasy and romance spanning four thousand years, from pre-civilization to contemporary and beyond.

Visit A.L. Hawke at www.alhawke.com

Email: contact@alhawke.com